PLANETEERING

A Pedro the Water Dog Saves the Planet Primer

AVIS KALFSBEEK

This is a work of fiction. Names, characters, places, and incidents
are the product of the author's imagination or are used fictitiously.
Any resemblance to actual persons, living or dead, events, or locales is coincidental or
satirical. Some events described herein are similar to events that actually happened or, if
visionary and affirmative, describe perfectly possible events in the future.

Acknowledgments:
Jesse Ahmann, Montana Cellist - National Park Service Conservation
Livia Albick-Ripka - Patreon Patrons
Robert D. Bullard - Peach Tree Rascals
Benjamin Katz Creative - Kendra Pierre-Louis
Kate Messmer Jessup, Peace of Kate - Nadja Popovich
Ravi Singh and Ana Brett

ISBN 978-1-953965-03-5 (First Edition Hardback)
ISBN 978-1-953965-04-2 (First Edition Paperback)
ISBN 978-1-953965-05-9 (Ebook)

www.AvisKalfsbeek.com

For Judith Hageman Kalfsbeek

who reminds us to make love, not war

CHAPTER 1
WADDEN SEA NATIONAL PARK, DENMARK - 146,600 HA

(55.2423, 8.5089)

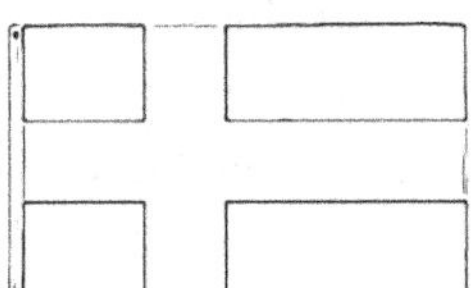

Immense regal windmills, taller than London's Big Ben, rotate in a long row over the bright blue North Sea off the coast of Denmark. On a brisk spring afternoon in a modern time when many say the world will eventually not sustain human life, from a bird's-eye view, three bicycles ride along a road through green rolling hills beneath the twirling blades of a wind farm. Tilly, a young woman in her late twenties, wholesomely pretty and fit, with long black hair and olive complexion, and her best friend Camas, a strong young woman in her twenties, with curly strawberry blond hair, freckles, a fit full-figure and one arm decorated in artistic tattoos, ride along the grounds of Frederiksborg Castle. Verdens Imorgen, a middle-aged Danish man with short brown hair, bleached blonde on the top, rides alongside in slim-fit plaid pedal pushers. He points out historical high points of the castle. The trio stops in front of the Baroque gardens, known as the Scandinavian Versailles.

"In the seventies, Denmark was paralyzed by oil prices and nearly shut down. People couldn't even heat their homes. The government moved quickly to make changes. Now we're leading the world in clean energy, including wind, solar, geothermal, and bioenergy," Verdens says proudly, standing over his bike.

"Bioenergy? Is that like burning cow pies in the wild wild west?" Camas asks.

"You mean dung cakes?"

"Yep."

"Probably similar. Our biofuels are made of manure, animal fats, and straw from agriculture."

"Shit power," Camas says, laughing.

Verdens smiles good-naturedly. "Anyway, we're honored to have your One More Year billboard in Copenhagen."

"We're excited to be launching the international One More Year tour in the greenest country in the world," Tilly responds.

"Danes have a high standard of living and with it a large carbon footprint. We can stand to be reminded to keep our stuff longer — to live a simpler life."

"Everyone can stand to be reminded." Tilly smiles.

They pedal on. Camas speeds up to ride alongside Tilly. "Ask your question," Camas says in a hushed voice.

Verdens overhears. "Shoot. I'm an open book."

"Respectfully, I'm curious why you wrote your book, The Eco Sceptic," Tilly says. "I know it's been over twenty years, but you were an environmentalist back then, as far as I can t...."

Camas butts in, "You pretty much became the poster boy of the climate deniers, and it took you ten years to change your tune. Did you do it to be controversial? To get on Letterman?"

Tilly gives her a stern look.

"There's room for controversy. Eisenweitz challenges the carbon credit model," Verdens responds.

"I think he's challenging the war model. I just wonder if, in this climate crisis, we shouldn't all be on the same team."

Verdens is quiet, thinking. "Didn't your brother, Moore, disparage the Ocean scoop-up Machine."

"Good research," Camas says, impressed.

"I saw the hip hop plastic video." He pauses, then speaks slowly. "Always remember, everything contains its opposite."

Tilly rides on, looking ahead somberly. "Do not seek the truth. Seek the spirit of truth."

"Pathway of Roses," Verdens says.

Tilly nods.

Camas shakes her head. She utters an unintelligible Chinese phrase under her breath.

"Excuse me?" Verdens asks.

"Confucius say, 'Man who makes mistake in elevator, wrong on many levels,'" she says with a Chinese accent.

A flock of birds swoops down over the vast water features of the gardens. Their wings make rhythmic ripples as they skim the surface of the glass-like ponds.

Screens in homes, pubs, airports, and gas stations display images of brown, raw sewage pouring into a large waterway within view of the Copenhagen skyline.

A Copenhagen reporter's voice says, "Swedish teenage climate activist Greta Thunberg lashed out at Copenhagen authorities on Wednesday because the city has for the last six years pumped 35 billion liters of wastewater into the strait separating Sweden and Denmark and plans to dump another 290,000 cubic meters in a few days."

CHAPTER 2

KAKADU NATIONAL PARK, AUSTRALIA – 1,980,400 HA

(-13.0876, 132.3931)

Four men in sleeveless wetsuits stand at the top of a cliff on a windy island off the coast of Tasmania, Australia. One by one, they climb into a five-foot-wide enclosed steel slide at the top of the bluff. They push off to glide down 100 feet and shoot out into the sea. They swim vigorously to a rope, then climb the vertical rock face of the island with the waves crashing below. They grimace as the early morning wind beats at them, climbing skillfully from ledge to crevice and crevice to ridge. Hare Finnish, a handsome, rugged man in his forties, reaches the top first and three young men in their early twenties, sons Buck, Garfield, and Jamie, arrive shortly after. The men shake hands firmly, then run vigorously along a beautiful, jagged coastline trail.

A weathered, sturdy stone house and lighthouse sit in the middle of the island. A warm orange light shines from the windows in the early morning. The father and sons rush into the house. They pull off their wetsuits and quickly change into pants and jerseys. Hare kisses his wife, Felice, her long blonde hair extending over the top of a floral apron. He sits down at a table full of eggs, smoked bacon, grilled tomatoes and mushrooms, hash browns, beans, and thick toast arranged around a small bouquet of wildflowers and set with well-used linen napkins. Felice kisses the young men and sits down with them to say a quick blessing. She stands, takes her apron off, and runs out the door and across the field to parasail off the island cliff.

"Finish your breakfast and run down to the boat to retrieve your mum," Hare says as he spreads Vegemite on his toast.

Tilly and Camas run fast through a forest outside of Stockholm. They turn and jump to maneuver the forest landscape, each holding a map and compass.

"Framåt!" Camas yells as she charges on in the lead. She looks down at her compass again, then up, "Framåt!"

They turn a corner and come out into a meadow. Tilly picks up speed to run alongside Camas.

Camas looks at her compass again, adjusts course a bit. "Framåt!"

"What in the world are you saying?!" Tilly says as they jig, jag, and jump over tree trunks, rocks, and small streams.

"'Onward' in Swedish. Surprised you don't know it, worldly woman that you are."

"Nope." Tilly laughs. "And speaking of the planet, fräulein, how in the world did we end up in this race?"

"Fräulein is not PC, sista, or Swedish."

"School me."

"It's outdated, diminutive, and there's no male equivalent."

"I stand corrected. Are you retaliating because I called you out on in Denmark about the equally non-PC Confucius joke?" Tilly asks.

"Maybe." Camas laughs.

Runners wearing colorful running attire and race numbers pinned to their shirt fronts emerge from the forest into the meadow. They move quickly, maps and compasses in hand. Indistinct, urgent shouts are heard from the galloping athletes.

Camas turns and sees them. She picks up speed. "Framåt, flicka!"

"Framating!" Tilly yells, following close behind.

Tilly runs along the city streets of Stockholm, then up the stairs of an old vine-covered brick building. She comes out with rolled-up papers in her hand and runs down the street. She arrives to the Riksdag, the seat of the parliament of Sweden, where a hoard of people and an interviewer stand around Greta Thunberg. Greta sits on the sidewalk with a "Skolstrejk för klimatet" sign painted on a large poster board. Tilly waits, jogging in place for a few minutes and tries to peer into the group to see Greta. Tilly answers a phone call, looks at her watch, and runs off with a disappointed look.

Greta looks up and sees her. She stands up and calls, "Tilly!"

With music playing through earbuds, Tilly doesn't hear and runs on.

A clear, strong voice pierces through the rumbles of a peacefully assembled crowd in Lafayette Square with the United States Capitol in the distance. "Don't it always seem to go that you don't know what you've got till it's gone? They took paradise and put up a fracking site."

Protesters of all ages, colors, and walks of life follow along with the folksong to the melody of Joni Mitchell's Big Yellow Taxi. "Don't it always seem to go," they sing loudly in unison, voices harmonizing, "you don't know what you got till it's gone? They took paradise and put up a fracking site! Ooh, la, la, la!"

The demonstrators carry oversized skeletons of extinct animals and wear artful badges of makeup, costumes, and T-shirts. Handmade-Tale-like *red rebel brigade* in geisha-white face with red cloaks and flags, fuzzy-knit pussy hats, Black Lives Matter T-shirts, Sierra Club Birkenstocks, a floating octopus, ESP hourglass patches, sounds of recorded animal calls floating behind the chanting, create a womb of sacred energy in defense of all living things on the planet.

Sarah Montana, a pretty, fair-skinned, waif-like young woman in her twenties, with wire-rimmed glasses, wearing a flowing bohemian-style skirt, scarves, and a colorful stack of bracelets jingling on her slim wrist, carries a sign reading *Extinction Rebellion. Climate Justice Now!*

CHAPTER 3
PAPAHĀNAUMOKUĀKEA MARINE NATIONAL MONUMENT, UNITED STATES - 151,000,000 HA

(25.7277, 170.4549)

Dark clouds roll over a group of men in cricket whites.

"Last hour!" the umpire calls.

Hare, Buck, Garfield, Jamie, and the other players walk off the field in joyful camaraderie. Fremont Fonear, Hare's best friend and manager, runs to catch up, his flannels snug over his short, well-built body.

"Saved by the weather! I thought we were going to beat the 1939 timeless test record for longest match," Fremont says sarcastically.

"You suggested timeless, cobber."

"Only to be able to talk with you. When you're out here, I can't even get a text to you."

"That's why I love it!"

Hare smiles at his wife, Felice, sexy in her wetsuit and helmet as she rolls a cart of sandwiches, cakes, pies, crisps, and hot tea over to the edge of the field.

After tea, the cricketers board two large, motorized life rafts with Buck and Jamie at the steering tillers.

Fremont stands on the dock next to Hare. "I've been trying to get the location of the big race from you for weeks. You've got to make a decision."

Hare laughs.

"I mean it, Hare! I've got sponsors breathing down my neck."

"I invited you for a match, Fremont, not to work."

"Throw me a bloody bone."

Hare shakes his head and smiles.

Fremont boards the raft. "I need the location of the race by next week!"

Buck and Jamie start the engines.

Hare turns around and shouts over the engine noise, "Ten national parks in the states!"

"Did you know that this entire time?!"

Hare smiles.

"We'll never get approval for that!"

"Get off your fat date and get to work on it. And we're rebranding the name. I want climate in the title, mate!"

Hare bends down and unties the boats from the dock.

"And it's going to be Score-O!" Hare calls as he turns to walk up the steep rocky trail.

"That'll be too expensive to follow the teams on different routes!"

The motors rev, and the rafts head away.

Hare turns back around. "One more thing. We'll end at the Grand Canyon!"

"Bastard!"

Fremont puts his phone to his ear, then looks down at it. He taps and taps, then shoves it in his pocket, frustrated. He gives Hare a dramatic Italian salute, placing his left hand on his right bicep, then swinging the firmly melded fingers of his right hand upwards.

Hare laughs and continues up the hill.

Durga Gelderland, an outdoorsy woman in her mid-forties with blonde shoulder-length hair wearing hiking boots and khaki shorts, speaks to a small group of people as she stands along the iron railing of the Yuvapai Geology Museum over the West Rim of the Grand Canyon.

"During Forty-Five's presidency, nearly 19 million acres of public land has been offered up for oil and gas leasing, and 24 million acres have proposals to slash their conservation protections by eighty percent. The Bureau of Land Management has been hijacked, and only a Green Amendment can provide the protections for our national parks and the treasured landscapes that surround them."

The crowd applauds.

Durga holds up a pamphlet. "Together, let's read the proposed Green Amendment for Arizona! 'The people have a right to pure water, clean air, a stable climate, healthy environments and to the preservation of the natural, scenic, historic and aesthetic values of the environment." Durga recites by memory as the crowd reads along from their phones and pamphlets. "'Arizona's public natural resources are the common property of all the people, including generations yet to come. As trustee of these resources, the State shall conserve and maintain them for the benefit of all the people.'"

The hoarse, long whistle-scream of a red-tail hawk fills the nearby canyon.

CHAPTER 4
NORTHEAST GREENLAND
NATIONAL PARK, GREENLAND –
97,200,000 HA

(76.0000, -30.0000)

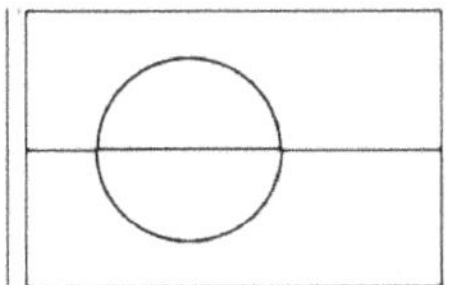

Sarah and other poetry reading attendees sit in rows under a tall ceiling of colorful circular art and mobiles in the center of Mies van der Rohe's Martin Luther King Jr. Memorial Library. She looks around the immense library and leans over from her chair to grab a book off a nearby shelf.

A black woman with glasses walks to the front of the room. Kara Jackson's lustrous braids shine like silk-threaded cords on a castle's brocade curtain. "My poems open one eye during grace, my poems stroke the spine of the sobbing, my poems have lost a best friend, have buried her on a nipping December, and still my poems wake up, even at noon, even just to see the last wink of the sun, if it means they are still alive, just for that day, my poems have done enough."

The crowd applauds loudly.

Librarian Judy, an older woman with short white hair, claps as she walks to the front, smiling kindly. "Thank you, Kara. What an honor to have you here in Washington D.C. from Oak Park, Illinois. Next up is Thomas Foolerin."

There is polite, less energetic applause from the audience.

Thomas, a young black man with short bleached-blonde hair, hurries to the front of the room. He wears an elaborate costume of an ancient East Indian mystic, a long red silk jacket with gold details, a green silk underlayer, curled tip shoes, and a white turban. A fake black goatee is pasted to his chin.

Thomas turns on a small speaker, and the beat of a Bolly-wood-inspired song fills the room.

"Is the sweetness of the cane sweeter than the one who made the canefield?" Thomas recites.

Sarah looks up from her book. "Hmmm... Rumi," she says under her breath.

"A small body of determined spirits fired by an unquench-able faith in their mission can alter the course of history."

Sarah tilts her head as she listens. Thomas notices her from across the room.

"Behind the beauty of the moon is the moon maker."

Thomas pauses.

"An eye for an eye only ends up making the whole world blind."

"Ah, and Gandhi," Sarah says quietly.

An older woman in front of Sarah turns around and frowns. Sarah shrugs.

"There is intelligence inside the ocean's intelligence, feeding our love like an invisible waterwheel."

Thomas pauses between phrases, the beat of the Bolly-wood melody and Hindi lyrics lifting the ancient spoken words to the upper stacks.

"Even if you are a minority of one, the truth is the truth."

"There is a skill to making cooking oil from the olive tree."

"I am prepared to die, but there is no cause for which I am prepared to kill."

"Consider now the knack that makes eyesight, from the shining jelly-marble of your eyes."

"It's the action, not the fruit of the action, that's important. You have to do the right thing. It may not be in your power, may not be in your time, that there'll be any fruit. But that doesn't mean you stop doing the right thing. You may never know what results come from your action. But if you do nothing, there will be no result."

Thomas turns off the music and smiles in Sarah's direction. The crowd looks confused but applauds politely. Sarah applauds vigorously, sitting up very straight.

Thomas and Sarah walk slowly up the spiral staircase in the middle of the library. Thomas is awkward as he tries to match the pace of Sarah's steps.

"I liked your spoken-word piece, the Rumi Ghandi Bollywood mix," Sarah says shyly.

"Thanks! I'm not sure people knew what to make of it."

"Tres avant garde."

"You speak French?"

She laughs. "No, but I like French."

"I like French too," Thomas says sweetly. "What are you doing in DC?"

"I'm working for Senator Mesopelagic."

"Of course, the Refill bill. I'm surprised we haven't bumped into each other on the hill. I'm a lobbyist."

Sarah scrunches her nose in distaste, "Aw, no." She quickly corrects herself. "Whoops, I'm sorry."

"It's OK. I'm on the good side. I lobby all things green."

"Oh, thank goodness, because you're adorable... oh, I didn't mean to say that out loud either. Must be this library," she says, looking down at the library from the balcony. "Or your outfit."

They turn around and see a large painting of Martin Luther King Jr. with a quote underneath.

"I have a personal question for you. Well, three, actually."

"I'm an open book," Thomas says, his arms outstretched to the book stacks.

"The first question is who do you work for?"

"I work for different people, but for the last few years, I've primarily worked for the godfather of the constitution, Olivier Clan."

"I thought the godfather was James Madison."

"He was the father," Thomas says gently. "Olivier is the godfather. He wields it."

"Do you have a girlfriend?"

Thomas takes a deep breath, emboldened. "The answer is no unless she's standing right here."

Sarah looks downward, smiling. "My third question is how would you feel about reading aloud to me?"

Thomas gently lifts her hand, bends down on one knee, kisses it gently, then guides her to a chair to sit. He stands up straight in front of the MLK Jr. painting and reads the passage.

"Here and there, an individual or group dares to love and rises to the majestic heights of moral maturity."

Sarah's eyes are wide as she listens.

The quote on the wall reads,

So in a real sense this is a great time to be alive... Granted that we face a world crisis which leaves us standing so often amid the surging murmur of life's restless sea. But every crisis has both its dangers and its opportunities. It can spell either salvation or doom. In a dark confused world, the kingdom of God may yet reign in the hearts of men.

Thomas rhyme-phrases and adlibs the last part of the passage,

"This is a great time to be alive, standing in life's restless sea. Every crisis holds dangers and hopes, but with hopeful hearts open, sets us free."

"Hey, you changed Dr. King's words," Sarah smiles.

"I did. I like rhyming. And I like you." Thomas looks tenderly at Sarah as he takes her hand and leads her to stand.

CHAPTER 5
YUKON DELTA NATIONAL WILDLIFE REFUGE, CANADA - 7,753,800 HA

(61.3670, -163.7170)

Bernard Lonely, Interior Secretary and head of the Bureau of Land Management, a grey-haired, stocky man in his early fifties, stands over a conference table covered with a map of the United States with large areas shaded in dark green.

"These are the federal lands with mining opportunities," Bernard says, pointing to the map.

"I thought those conservationists, Orvis-wearin' sportsmen, and Artemis huntresses were all up in arms and killed Chaffetz's bill to sell off three million acres of this Western public land," says Henry 'Hank' Chimiker, the CEO of Sascartoon, one of the largest uranium mining companies in the world.

"They did, so we're going stealth instead—no broad policies. POTUS says divide and conquer. I'm authorized to put nearly everything west of the Mississippi up for lease with some land as low as $2 an acre."

"We might be interested in the uranium. We'll definitely make a bid on all of the oil and gas stakes," says Chimiker.

"Don't try to act nonchalant about the uranium, Hank.

I'm sure you got a call from the White House Nuclear Fuel Working Group just like we did." Maus Back, of Zag Energy, a small man with a high squeak of a voice, says.

Hank clears his throat and looks the other way.

"Uranium aside, why don't you take the oil, and we'll take gas," Maus suggests.

"Maybe Bitumines wants all of them?" Goosey says. She wears clunky costume jewelry, a silk top, and jeans.

"When you were in prison, your father told me he wants to stay focused on coal," Hank says.

"Well, I'm not in prison anymore, now am I?" Goosey says flirtatiously. "If everyone says fossil fuels will be dinosaurs — that's ironic now, isn't it," she snorts a laugh, "we can't rely on just one of them."

"I don't understand why you've brought us all here together when you could have just offered up the various lands to create a bidding war," Hank says.

"Who's to say that you can't start a bidding war here?" Bernard laughs heartily. "I asked you all here because a group strategy is needed if we truly want to get access to these resources with the least resistance as possible."

A woman's voice is heard just outside the door. "You mean, you don't want any Sienna Club eco-freak tree huggers coming around to spoil all the fun?" Reina McCaring, Deputy Directory of the Environmental Protection Agency, a young woman in her thirties with short, wavy blond hair and black-framed glasses, walks through the door.

CHAPTER 6
PHOENIX ISLANDS PROTECTED AREA, REPUBLIC OF KIRIBATI – 40,825,000 HA

(-3.6497, -172.8574)

Tall, sawtooth, glacier-formed mountains soar over a slow-moving section of the Lewis Fork River outside Sandglass. A stocky, muscular, red-haired man in boat shoes and a kilt sits atop a kayak paddling smoothly through the water. He has red hair on the center of his chest, a Celtic knot tattoo on his upper back, a handlebar mustache, and wears a wide-banded watch and a brown tweed newspaper-boy-style flat cap.

"Lassies, care to see my bagpipes?!" Cashal calls out in his Scottish accent to three young women floating ahead of him in inner tubes. The women, wearing shorts, colorful bikini tops, and ball caps, turn around with confused looks. They quickly turn away to talk among themselves.

"Hey, Bonnies. How about a beer, then? I'm thirsty after all this paddling. Give a dry Scotsman a cold one, will ya?"

One of the women reluctantly pulls a beer out of an ice chest carried by their fourth tube and throws it to Cashal. He opens it and puts his mouth over the foaming beer.

"Don't want to miss a drop now, do we?" Cashal paddles

closer. "I'm a seaman. We never want to neglect the wee baby fishies."

The women try to paddle away, but Cashal's kayak gains on them.

Cashal takes another swig of the beer. "Thanks for the beer. My bagpipes are just under..." he says as he points to a tattoo on his upper thigh and starts to raise his kilt.

"Hey, Cashal! Come this way to see some river otters!" Reeve, a handsome man in his late forties with salt and pepper hair, interrupts, attempting to save the girls.

Reeve and Cutter, whose kayaks have a compass and map on the front, watch Cashal as he reluctantly paddles back in their direction.

Cutter, 6'2" in his early thirties with red hair and a beard, says, "I may not be first-generation Scot, but somewhere along the line, I learned when to keep my kilt down."

"Aww, they're fine. I'm getting' auld, not young like you Cutter, and only have a few times left to get my dobber out."

"Common guys. Let's train," Reeve says, paddling strongly ahead. "Cashal, you're up to find the next control point."

Cashal finishes the beer, pulls a map and compass from between his legs, gives the young women a wave, and paddles ahead.

CHAPTER 7

GALAPAGOS MARINE RESERVE, ECUADOR – 14,600,000 HA

(-0.3333, -90.0000)

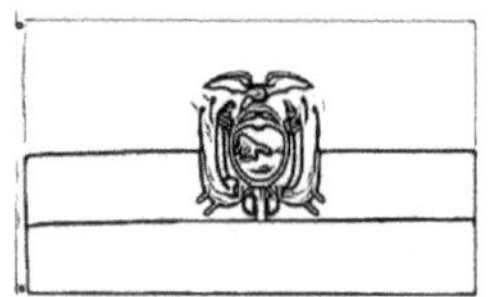

Camas and Tilly take a break from One More Year billboard launch obligations in the tranquil oasis of Djurgården royal park, Stockholm.

Camas sings and dances to "Dancing Queen" at the ABBA Museum.

Tilly and Camas ride the merry-go-round at Gröna Lund amusement park.

The young women stop and smell the colorful roses at Rosendals Trädgård public garden.

Camas and Tilly dance a traditional Swedish Hambo at Prince Eugen's former home, Waldemarsudde, an elegant art museum.

Tilly exits Skaansen Bakery with a bag of warm cinnamon buns.

"The prince lives here!" Camas says, pointing at Blockhusudden, Prince Carl Philip's current home. "Let's knock!"

"Let's sit and eat our kardemummabullar," Tilly says as she sits down on the grass overlooking the water. She walks over to look closely at a beautiful statue of a woman with flowing hair, arms outstretched. "She's the *lady working for peace in the world,* and she's standing on the Nobel Peace Prize," Tilly calls over to Camas.

"Very pretty, but she needs a cinnamon bun. I got the kanelbullar," Camas says with her mouth full. "They get you addicted to the cinnamon rolls at IKEA, so you have to travel to Sweden to get the real thing."

"Since when do you go to IKEA?"

"Like never if I want to be your friend. I just say no to disposable."

Tilly laughs. "That's my girl."

"Great billboard launch. Fantastic job, sista!"

"You too. It seemed to go OK considering we don't speak Swedish."

A tall, handsome blonde man in athletic running clothes passes by with a map and compass in his hand. He spots Camas and stops abruptly.

"Camas!"

"Oh, hi, Otto!"

Tilly is surprised. "Hi?"

"Oh, sorry, this is my best friend, Tilly. What are you searching for around here?"

"We have a city club that orienteers for anything and everything. There are over 3,000 control points in Stockholm," he says with a Swedish accent. He pretends to match his map to her cinnamon roll. "No, not there!" he jokes, standing close to her.

Camas laughs flirtatiously. She stands up and talks with Otto out of earshot of Tilly. Tilly rolls her eyes. She watches them for a minute, then becomes impatient, pacing.

Finally perturbed, "Hey, we've got a train to catch," Tilly says, tapping Camas's arm.

"We have two hours un..."

Tilly interrupts, "No, remember we need to do that thing I mentioned earlier?" giving Camas the let's get out of here look.

Camas reluctantly pulls away from Otto, "Hey, thanks for the orienteering lesson. It paid off."

"Yes, I hear you did well on the first try."

The friends turn and walk away as Otto runs off, face down towards his map.

"So that explains the sudden interest in orienteering -- the handsome Swede."

"You were taking a run and visiting the Stockholm Environmental Institute, and I went for a Swedish pastry 'run,'" Camas defends. "Otto asked if he could sit next to me, and I said OK. He told me about orienteering, and I thought it sounded fun. I like running, and I like making tactical decisions."

"And you make great ones. You've built up One More Year like you have a Ph.D. in tactics," Tilly says, "but what about Josh?"

"I told him about it that night on the phone, and he said it was no big deal."

"That's good you told him."

"I'm not a two-faced slut, Till."

"I know," Tilly says, hugging her.

"I just don't know if Josh cares about me if he wasn't even a tiny bit jealous," Camas says. She looks up over Tilly's shoulder. "Let's run! There's our shuttle!"

Camas and Tilly talk and laugh, sitting side by side on a train through Stockholm.

"You need high physical qualities, endurance, strength, and sturdiness to run in the forest, a perfect exploiting of the map, a rapid decidedness," Camas reads.

"Your CFO job description?"

"It's an orienteering book, silly,"

"I know," Tilly smiles. "I was just following you in the forest. How do you navigate in the middle of nowhere?"

"Funny you should ask," Camas says proudly, pulling a compass and map from her backpack.

"Looks like you're ready to framåt anywhere."

"Damn right, sista. OK. All you need to remember on this compass is that it points north."

"What about all those other gizmos? The mirror, the site, the other dials?"

"Just bullshit extras. You look at where the needle is pointing and orient the map. That's it."

"That's it?"

"Well, then you look at the psychedelic lines, colors, and shapes on the map and find an attack point."

"What's an attack point?"

"It's a feature you can run to fast — faster than if you're

navigating to the control point — like a kink in a trail or a creek crossing or a change from a meadow to a forest. Then once you get to the attack point, you can navigate to the more remote control point."

"So even if it isn't as direct, it's faster in the end."

"*Exakt*. I assume it's an attack point because orienteering was part of military training. It didn't become a competitive sport in Sweden until 1919."

"It could be called the vantage point," Tilly offers.

"Can we tackle climate before we try to reform orienteering?"

"OK." Tilly laughs.

Camas demonstrates. "And if you place your thumb on your current location on the map and move it as you run, you'll maneuver faster too."

"And I thought I was the nerdy one. Any other tips?"

Camas points out the window to the One More Year billboard as they pass by. "Only 'Ett År Till, håll dina saker längre.'"

Tilly puts her arm around her best friend and smiles. "Let's."

CHAPTER 8

GREAT LIMPOPO TRANSFRONTIER PARK, SOUTH AFRICA, MOZAMBIQUE & ZIMBABWE - 3,500,000 HA

(-22.4333, 31.3666)

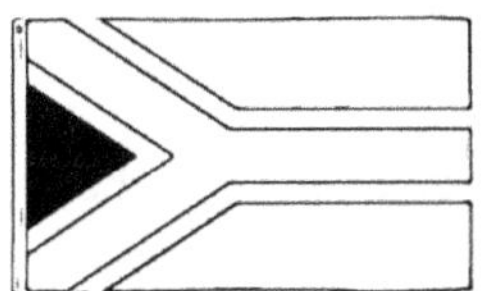

Tilly and Camas orienteer with a map and compass in hand past a majestic waterfall in Iceland, the land of fire and ice.

The smell of warm Kjötsupa, traditional lamb meat soup, wafts over Tilly and Camas's table in the cozy pub, Micro Bar, in Reykjavik.

Camas takes a drink of beer. "You're eating the baby sheep."

"I gave up 'meatless six-days' for 'meatless seven-days' a year ago, but the orienteering race and this cozy pub, and your bad influence," Tilly glares, "pulled me down. And it's lamb, by the way."

"I know. Those sheep looked pretty darn happy in that pasture, though."

"They did. Until today." Tilly pushes the bowl away. She puts butter on a thin slice of dark rye bread and takes a bite.

Camas quickly pulls Tilly's bowl towards her, dips her spoon in, and takes a big slurp. With her mouth full, "And why are we in Iceland again? There's no population here. Don't get me wrong. I enjoyed the race," she looks over to a neighboring table of four men and smiles, "and the guys are cute."

"Who's cute?" Otto says as he walks up, his large frame taking up nearly half the cozy pub.

"Otto! Hey!" Camas says as she stands and hugs him. "How'd you do today?"

"I took second place."

The Icelander beefcakes turn their attention away from Camas and frown. Tilly raises her eyebrows.

"Have a seat," Camas says. "Tilly, you remember Otto."

"Hi, Otto," Tilly says perfunctorily. To Camas, "To answer your question, we're in Iceland because One More Year is about controlling consumption to slow CO_2 and Iceland is one of the most environmentally advanced countries on the planet. There's also someone I want to meet."

"Who's that?"

"Her name's Perla Seruma."

"What's her claim to fame?" Camas asks.

"She's the Prime Minister of Climate Change," one of the Icelander hunks in an olive green down jacket says.

"And *the* Prime Minister," Otto adds, puffing his chest.

Testosterone breaks through the ice like the degraded melting permafrost. "Yes, and the Emma Peale of Prime Ministers," green-puff-jacket man adds. "She's in her eighties now, but back in the '6os, she was hot! She was even in a black and white music video in a miniskirt."

"Sounds cool!" Camas says. To Tilly, "You know I have to get back to Sandglass. We've outgrown our shoebox office, and I've got the non-profit application to finish."

"Yes, I know, and you need to get home to Josh," she says pointedly, looking at Otto.

"Yes, back to Josh," Camas says, looking down as she takes a big drink of beer.

Otto and the four guys at the table next door look very disappointed, shrug their shoulders, and take a swig of beer.

Tilly and Camas stand outside their small hotel in quaint downtown Reykjavik. Bright red, green, and blue roofs on the A-frame buildings surround them with a view of the glass-domed, spaceship-like Perlan Museum in the distance.

"Please be safe on the rest of the tour. Hopefully, we'll have new digs when you get back."

"Thanks for taking care of that," Tilly says as she hugs her. "I'll be safe. You travel safely too."

"I sent you your contacts in all the cities."

"Got them. I miss you already," Tilly hugs Camas again.

Camas gets into a taxi.

CHAPTER 9
CABRERA ARCHIPELAGO
MARITIME-TERRESTRIAL
NATIONAL PARK, SPAIN –
90,800 HA

(39.1513, 2.9337)

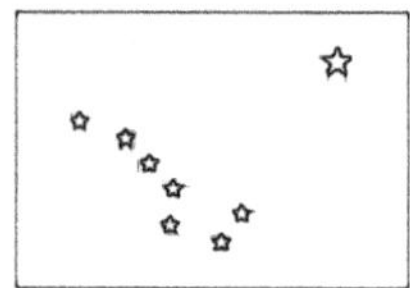

Bernard, Goosey, Henry, and Maus turn to look towards the door.

"McCaring, what are you doing here?" Bernard says, surprised.

"I had to be in Colorado for a wedding, so I thought I'd stop by and congratulation you on your new offices."

"You could have called first," he says rudely.

"Oh, that wouldn't have been nearly so fun, and look at the party I would have missed!"

"Why don't we grab a coffee later."

"Oh no, you all go on. I'll just sit in. I'm sure I'll find it fascinating." McCaring walks over to join the group and looks down at the map on the table. "These are the crown jewels of each of these states," Reina says with disgust. "Every gas and oil lease you sign, Bernie, is the systematic dismantling of the Department of the Interior and the BLM. It's like you're pulling out the blocks of a Jenga tower until it collapses."

"And?" Bernard responds impatiently.

"POTUS wants us to be an energy leader, but why don't

we become an energy leader in renewable energy." She looks pointedly at the group. "Fossil fuels are a time bomb. You all know petroleum's finished. You can only look for other opportunities, like shoving plastic down Africa's throat, for so long. Petrochemicals may be the last man standing for you. Still, most sane people in this world are quitting plastic packaging and pesticides so that man won't be standing for long."

"McCaring, to be honest, darling, I know you're young and idealistic, so we'll be kind..." Bernard says, "...these lands have a best use, and that's profits, not trails for some hairy-legged hikers or hippies in their broken-down Scooby-Doo mystery vans."

"Why chase after these resources?" Reina says, exasperated.

Goosey turns her nose up at Reina. "Bernie, Forty-Five told me he would be so happy if we bid on all the lands, and that's what we're going to do."

"Good luck, Goosey. The Umpaloompa may ack like he makes all the decisions, but Bernard is where the buck stops. May the best bid win," Hank challenges.

"Rumor has it, Bernard, that you moved BLM out here to Colorado from DC to sell oil and gas leases. Who'd have believed it? You know who? Ruh roh. A bunch of hairy-legged hikers."

Bernard makes a loud grunt of disgust, "Arghhh."

"And I hope they hike right in here and shove that map up your oil and gas ass. Good day, have a good meeting," Reina says as she nods to Hank, Maus, and Goosey, "Tyrannosaurs Rex, Troodon and Velociraptor."

Reina glances down at the map and sees an area shaded at the South Rim of the Grand Canyon. She turns to Bernard, "I'll let my boss know I checked in on you, Spine-lesssaurus." She slams the door behind her as she walks out.

"Bitch," Bernard says distastefully.

"Are we done here, Bernie?" Goosey asks. "I'm going to my chalet in Aspen and to get a facial. I'm feeling a little scaly," she jokes, holding the backs of her hands up to her face.

"Yes, just one more thing. A TV producer called me to do some kind of adventure expedition at a few national parks. I told him to fuck off."

"Good work. We don't need more attention on the parks," Maus squeaks.

CHAPTER 10

SELOUS GAME RESERVE, TANZANIA - 5,460,000 HA

(-7.7545, 38.2355)

Camas runs through Sherwood Forest outside of Sandglass with a map and compass. She wears headphones and adds dance moves to the beat as she runs and jumps. Reeve runs on a nearby trail and sees Camas moving expressively in the forest. He smiles.

"Hey, Camas!"

Camas doesn't hear him.

Reeve picks up his bike, puts it over his shoulder, and runs off the trail toward her. "Hey!" he shouts again.

Camas finally sees him and stops, "Hi, Reeve!"

"Welcome home! How was the trip? We saw you a couple of times on the news."

"It was great. Tilly stayed on. Well, that's a long story that I'll tell you about over a beer some time, and I'm back home searching for an office space for One More Year."

"I heard there's a space for rent over the rowing club."

"Really? That's a cool old building. Thanks. I'll check it out."

"Where did you learn to use the map and compass?"

"The birthplace of orienteering," she says with a Swedish accent.

Reeve laughs. He pauses, thinking. "We just formed an adventure racing team and need a female athlete. Want to join us?"

"I don't even know what that is. Wouldn't you rather have Tilly? She's the triathlete."

"One criterion is strength. Another is endurance. You seem to have a lot of both!"

"Thanks!" Camas says, flexing her bicep, smiling.

"I'll send you a video to watch because it can be pretty intense, but if you like a challenge, it's one of the most exciting sports out there."

"I'm game!"

"You know Big Cutter, and the other guy on the team is a Scotsman named Cashal. He's a little rough around the edges but has a good heart."

"Cool."

"We'll be training tomorrow out on Presta Island if you can make it."

"Sounds great. Text me the deets."

Camas takes off running with her map and compass, still dancing. "Framåt!"

Reeve laughs and carries his mountain bike back to the trail. He climbs on, then stands up to pedal powerfully up the hill.

CHAPTER 11

CENTRAL KALAHARI GAME RESERVE, BOTSWANA – 5,200,000 HA

(-21.8895, 23.7565)

Tilly walks along the coast with Perla Seruma, a slender woman in her eighties with white hair pulled back in a ponytail. Perla wears a white wool cap, jeans, boots, and an off-white Icelandic wool sweater with a round patterned design around the neck and shoulders.

"Your country's idyllic," Tilly says.

"Thank you. It is beautiful. Come, let's Ísbíltúr."

"He's bit tour?"

"Ísbíltúr. It's pronounced *ease-beel-tour*, and it's an Icelandic road trip to get ice cream."

"I love ice cream!"

"Great. It's a cultural phenomenon here."

They wind through the city with several stops for Perla to visit with citizens. She asks a young girl about her sick mother, gives an older man a phone number of a dog walker, answers questions about an upcoming community meeting, and congratulates a teenager for her thoughtful online comments.

"She sure looked happy after speaking with you!" Tilly says.

"We have a unique public forum that allows people to debate community and other issues."

"In my country, people do that all day long on social media."

"They do here as well, and many times it becomes a bitter battle of 'he said she said' in one topic one-liners. To participate in our forum known as Better Reykjavík, they must abide by some simple rules."

"What rules?"

"Rather than replying to each other one on one, citizens must list arguments for and against ideas."

"Interesting. How has that worked out?"

"It slows participation because we're asking them to evaluate the idea, not write the first thing they think of, but we get thoughtful discourse instead of fury clicks. Some fantastic ideas have come out of it. You may have heard of our 2009 pots and pans revolution in front of the parliament. We started the forum to restore public trust in our political process. Now it's more of a town square. More than twenty countries are using some version of it."

They arrive at an ice cream shop with a large bright red and white swirl ice cream cone painted on the front window. Once cozy inside, people wait patiently to order a cone or cup. An island of beautiful candy, crumbled cookies, fruit, and nuts is in the center of the room. Tilly orders salted licorice ice cream on a cone. Perla orders a blended Bragðarefur with almonds, dark chocolate chips, and crumbled almond-caramel Swedish Daim bars. Tilly pays for their ice cream, and they step back out onto the street.

"I'm so impressed that ninety-nine percent of your energy is hydropower and geothermal. Also, that Iceland is ranked first in gender equality," Tilly says.

Perla laughs. "If that were true, I'd be the thirteenth Prime Minister, not the twenty-eighth. But yes, we have made progress. Please tell me why you are here."

"Our organization One More Year asks people to curb their consumption and not buy so many new things. As you know, we have a billboard going up by your airport. I'm visiting the top green countries which have all signed on for a billboard too."

"Why are you only visiting the greenest countries?" Perla asks gently.

"That's an interesting question." Tilly pauses, thinking. "I suppose I don't know the answer."

Perla continues walking.

"What are the least green countries?" Tilly asks, hurrying to catch up to the elegant matriarch.

"Of course, there are many, but a recent report names Liberia, Myanmar, Afghanistan, Sierra Leone, and Cote d'Ivoire as the bottom five."

"Hmmm..." Tilly takes another lick of her ice cream cone.

Sarah walks into Senator Mesapologic's office. The Oregon Senator has a framed *Refill, Bill* poster of Plastic, the pug, in a cape on his wall. She puts a file down on his desk, then straightens the poster. She begins to say something, then stops. She opens her mouth to speak, then stops again.

"Sarah, is there something on your mind?"

She blurts out, "Can we write a bill for a green amendment?"

"We have a lot on our plate right now. The Refill bill needs to have our full attention to make sure it has teeth and gets implemented. We've got the energy efficient manufacturing bill, and the community first policing act, the..."

"I'm sorry to interrupt, sir. I know the work. I'm writing a lot of it for you."

"Of course. I just don't know how we'll fit something new in."

"Climate is one of the key platforms of your political career."

"Hmmm... I still don't know."

"Can I just get your OK to meet with Olivier Clan? I didn't want to meet with him without your approval. Can we get your blessing for that meeting?"

"Who's 'we'?"

"Thomas Foolerin."

"The young lobbyist. Got it. Where are you meeting Clan?"

"Harvard."

"So I guess you're asking me to pay to get you there?"

"The taxpayers. Yes, sir."

Reina walks through Grand Junction Regional Airport on her phone.

"How was your meeting at the BLM?" Reina's assistant asks.

"Prehistoric."

"Huh?"

"Let's just say that Director Bernard Lonely is no Karl Landstrom. Not only did BLM Director Landstrom reduce the backlog of land applications and pulled the reigns on what President Kennedy called uncontrolled land use, but he also championed Secretary of the Interior Udall's Third Conservation Wave and the philosophy that natural resources are finite, interrelated, and vulnerable components of larger systems." Reina's voice gets louder. "They were an era of environmental humanitarians! Now, we're in a time of environmental barbarians! Gluttonians!!"

"They don't eat wheat?"

"Oh God, no. They're gluttonous! Pillaging swindlers!"

"Reina, are you OK?"

"Call Senator Mesapoligic and find out the status of the Grand Canyon Protection Act."

"I can look it up. Hang on."

Reina waits.

"It says the bill was read twice and has been referred to the Committee on Energy and Natural Resources."

"Call him and ask for updated status. He's on that energy committee."

"OK. Will do. Also, besides withdrawing one million acres of federal lands around the Grand Canyon from mining, it says that 'The Government Accountability Office shall conduct a study of uranium stockpiles in the United States that are available to meet future national security requirements.'"

"Shit. Ask Mesopoligic what the hell that means."

"Doesn't it means they are studying the stockpiles?"

"What's there to study?! About 88 tonnes of plutonium and 560 tonnes of highly-enriched uranium. That could make about 60,000 new nuclear missiles by most calculations. Add to that the 5,000 existing warheads. So, I'm thinking we don't need any more uranium in the stockpile!"

"Or to *research* the stockpiles?"

"Bingo."

"I'll ask him."

CHAPTER 12

NAMIB-NAUKLUFT NATIONAL PARK, NAMIBIA – 4,976,800 HA

(-24.1667, 16.1667)

Reeve, Cutter, and Cashal step off Reeve's fishing boat and stand on the dock at Presta Island. There is a quaint log cabin several hundred yards away on the shoreline, but the remainder of the island is wooded and wild. The men look toward the water as they hear Camas motoring up in a 1950s era peach-colored atomic runabout boat.

Reeve helps her tie up and takes her hand as she climbs onto the dock. "You could have come with us."

"I'm headed over to see Graeme and Liz after, but thanks!"

"Is that a sail?" Reeve asks.

"Yeah. Tilly made me put it on because she didn't want to smell fuel or think about fuel when she trains. These already have so many fake things on them -- fake jet air intakes, fake jet exhausts, tail fins, T-bird style dash. I thought, what the hell? Let's throw a sail on her too!"

Reeve laughs. "Camas, you know Cutter. This is Cashal. Cashal, Camas."

"Hey, Cutter," Camas says, hugging him. She extends her hand to Cashal, and they shake firmly.

"Nice grip, Lassie," Cashal says, unsmiling.

Camas shrugs. "So what's this adventure stuff all about anyway?"

"Oh no," Cashal says gruffly, looking at Reeve. "You told me she was experienced."

"Camas knows orienteering. She trains with and coaches Tilly DeMontagne in her Ironman races. They did Banff and Kona Ironmans and then biked across the U.S. She's solid."

Camas looks perturbed. She puffs out her chest.

Cashal shakes his head. "Some call this the toughest sport on the planet. You look a bit too womanly to be good at it."

"Hey..." Reeve starts to say.

"It's OK, Reeve." Camas turns to address Cashal. "Listen, Lucky Charms welcome wagon, why don't you focus on your own training, and we'll see what we see. If you three decide I'm not up to par, or if I decide your karma is so off-kilter..." she laughs "kilt... er, get it?" Laughing at her joke, "then I and my womanliness will be on our way."

"I'm sure once we've been training for a bit, you'll be fast friends," Reeve says.

Cutter turns to Reeve and rolls his eyes skeptically. Cashal shrugs.

"Cutter, will you explain the basics as we warm up?"

"Sure! Did you watch the video Reeve gave you?" Cutter reaches up to stretch. Then down to his toes.

"Yeah."

"Great. The competitions are a series of different tasks, running, paddling, mountain biking, climbing, and even some other things that are complete surprises. Athleticism and endurance are key. You're strong and fast, Cam, and run long distances -- you'll be great."

Cashal grimaces.

"Then there's the tactical part," Cutter continues.

"I love that part!" Camas says excitedly. "My favorite game is Risk!"

Reeve smiles. "In a race, we need to quickly understand the map and find the best and quickest route to the next control point."

"First, you have to orient yourself," Cashal says. "I was once followin' a guy who didn't set his orientation, and we went in the opposite direction for two hours and lost four, the walloper!"

"Also, the straightest route as the crow flies could be the longest. For instance, it may be most direct to go over the hill in front of you, but that'll tire you out faster than if you go around. You need to plan your route to suit your physical capabilities for the entire race and the capabilities of the team," Cutter says.

"That part sounds just like orienteering," Camas says.

"That's right," Cutter answers.

"The hardest races are often Score-O. The "O" being orienteering. They don't give you the order of the control points. You have to figure that out for yourself."

"It sounds like a choose-your-own-adventure cross-country race!" Camas says.

"Exactly."

"Not quite." Cashal corrects. "It's more like a choose-to-have-someone-kick-your-ass-adventure race. They choose the course. Yes, we get to choose the route within in it, but it's all very ass-kickin' fun."

Cutter and Reeve nod.

"Today, we'll work on fitness and a bit of map reading," Reeve says. "Cutter and I talked about going to an adventure race clinic in Coeur d'Alene. Since I've only done cyclocross and alpine skiing, and Camas, it's your first time too, how does a class sound?"

"If we must," Cashal says with a heavy sigh. "You kick ass at cyclocross, by the way."

"Wow, a compliment," Camas teases. "Sounds great to me!"

"Thumbs up!" Cutter says.

Camas sits at Matchlove Brewery playing Risk with her boyfriend Josh, an athletic, young black man in his late twenties, with a short-trimmed beard.

"Damn. I don't remember this game being so violent as a kid."

"You don't remember that all the pieces are soldiers, cavalry, and artillery?" Josh questions.

"I was a kid."

"I bet you were an adorable kid," Josh says, kissing her.

"No wonder we're all so numb to war. We play war games in kindergarten."

"You played Risk in kindergarten?"

"No. I guess not. I was a cute little snowboarder and rode my bike. By middle school, though."

"Guess it's no different than the kids blowing people up in the video games."

"Aww, damn. You're right." Camas takes a big drink of beer with a worried face.

CHAPTER 13
LORENTZ NATIONAL PARK,
INDONESIA – 2,505,600 HA

(4.7500, 137.8333)

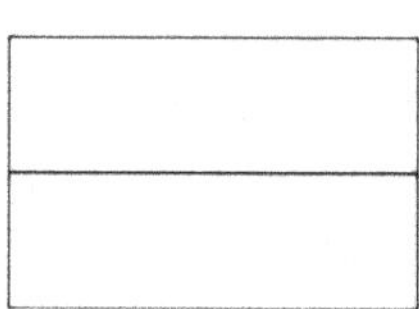

"Hello, Thomas!" Olivier says warmly as Thomas and Sarah enter his office. "And, who is this lovely lady?"

"Olivier, this is my... girlfriend," he smiles at Sarah, "Sarah Montana."

"Hello, Sarah. Have a seat, please. How do you like the campus?" Olivier asks.

"It is a dream to be here. So beautiful. I think I got smarter just walking through Harvard Yard."

"I bet you were plenty smart to begin with if you found Thomas."

Thomas smiles, "Thank you, sir."

"How can I help you today?"

"Mr. Clan, Thomas tells me you are the godfather of the Constitution, and I wanted to ask," she pauses, then says the rest very quickly, "if you will lead us to achieve a Green Amendment to the United States Constitution!"

Olivier's eyebrows raise. He looks at Thomas, then back to Sarah. "Well, well, now that's a project that will take more than an afternoon."

"Sir, I know, I know. It's a huge undertaking, but Thomas and I, and probably my mother, feel the timing is right."

"This undertaking is at least three lifetimes, and I have less than one quarter left, but you've piqued my curiosity. Why 'probably' your mother?"

"If you're the godfather of the constitution, my mother is the tooth fairy. She has been working at the state level to get green amendments to their bill of rights. She's diligent, and when people go to sleep, she flies in to give them a gift for what they've lost. She reminds them about their right to clean air, water, and a safe environment. Her name is Durga Gelderland."

"Durga! Aww, yes, of course. And you're right. She is diligent like the tooth fairy. She even gave me a gift once. I wrote an opinion that leaned a bit on the side of a coal company, and she mailed me an autographed copy of her Green Bill of Rights book along with a card that said, "Mistakes happen.""

"She is determined, but we just don't have time to go state by state, one at a time, when there is so much environmental devastation and the climate time bomb," Sarah says passionately.

"We would need...," Olivier starts.

Thomas and Sarah look at each other with a small smile because of his use of the word 'we.'

"... to get three-quarters of the states to pass the amendment, so her strategy is probably the best," Olivier says.

"What if there was something to bring the states on board in one fell swoop?"

"Like what?" Thomas asks.

"It would need to be populace led," Olivier says, thinking aloud.

"I think that goes without saying, sir," Sarah says.

Olivier looks at Thomas and smiles.

"Seems you have some ideas. Let me sleep on this. Meet me tomorrow at 8:00 am at Widener Library."

Thomas walks Sarah to her car. He kisses her on the cheek.

CHAPTER 14

CENTRAL KARAKORAM NATIONAL PARK, PAKISTAN – 1,055,700 HA

(35.9000, 75.5276)

Cashal sits in the passenger seat of Camas's Mini Cooper. Cutter's legs are over Reeve in the back seat..

"That was a boring pile of jobbies," Cashal grunts.

"I'm assuming jobbies isn't favorable," Camas says.

"It means shit," Cutter translates.

"Maybe next time they'll call to consult you, O Scottish lord of the isle of whiney bastards. I, on the other hand, learned a lot."

"Oh, you did, did ya? Well, you need to. What did you learn?"

"I learned that you have to be careful not to get hamburger foot...."

Cutter and Reeve grimace and nod.

"... and that the race will give us a list of mandatory gear that we can't deviate from."

"That's great, Camas. You rocked the clinic. I learned a few things, too," Reeve says.

"Mandatory gear also means the rulebook requirement to have at least one woman on a coed race," Cashal says.

"Thanks, Reeve," Camas says, giving Cashal a piercing you're-an-asshole-stare.

"Forget your hamburger foot. Where are you going to put your nice chebs when you have to run for fifty miles at a time?"

Camas scrunches her face. "Excuse me?"

"Cashal, cool it," Reeve says.

"I'm not even going to ask anyone to translate that," Camas says as she turns up the music and bops her head to the beat.

Hare, Felice, and their three sons raft down dramatic white-water on the Avon River in Western Australia. They laugh and shout in excitement as they row and bounce along.

Several miles downriver, Jamie and Buck pull the raft out of the water near a remote beach with four tents, a rock fire pit, and a camping table with a vase of greenery and wild-flowers from the surrounding terrain.

Hare pulls his phone out of his vest pocket. "Sorry, guys. It's Fremont." He runs up the bank and taps his phone.

"Did you get the parks?" He listens, then lets out a loud, "Whoop!"

Hare turns around to his family with a broad, handsome smile. "We're going to put on the greatest adventure race those seppos have ever seen, right in their backyard."

"Hare, that's not kind or PC. Those yanks pay our bills," Felice says.

"They're polluting, money mongering, brain dead morons."

"Dear!" Felice drops wood into the fire pit.

"And fat too," Hare adds.

"There are some pretty girls that aren't fat, Dad," Buck

says.

"And the men and women who are in your races are fit," Jamie adds.

"Well, a lot of those racers will be international, but yes, they have some talent. My Scot buddy, Cashel, is over there. He's not American, but he's in a yank team."

"And they have Huckleberries in the states," Buck says.

"I'm not sure I'd even call those natural places where the Huckleberries grow or their national parks part of their country. Most citizens never visit. They're home sitting on the couch watching TV. You go to a national park, and it's full of Europeans and Asians. And now they're dismantling the parks for mining."

"Since when do you care about U.S. politics," Jamie asks.

"Since they tried to stop the race. Fremont said we almost didn't get the parks because some mining companies tried to block it."

"How did you get it?"

"I told Fremont to tell the President of the United States he could ride down the rapids with your mother."

"You didn't." Felice shakes her head.

"I thought it was a small sacrifice for the superstars of the U.S. national parks system."

"OK, if it means that much to you, I can boat with Agent Orange for a couple of hours."

"Thank you, my love," Hare says, kissing her.

"Why are you so gung-ho on those parks, anyway? You could have picked some other remote place that would be lush and tropical. More Hollywood."

"I've been Hollywood these past twenty years. When my dad and I competed, he would design our expeditions, and they were straightforward and kick-ass hard. Now, it's all about the sponsors and the ratings. And our insurance makes sure we don't kill anybody."

"We get to live on an island all by ourselves because of it," Felice reminds him.

"I know. Sometimes I just feel like a cartoon character of myself. Hare, the mighty adventurer. The last true adventure I won was when I chased you through the Amazon to get you to marry me."

"I might have let you catch me," Felice says. They kiss deeply.

Reeve, Camas, Cashal, and Cutter eat a pizza listening to live Bluegrass music at Bijou Nez Winery. Camas and Reeve drink wine. Cutter and Cashal have Knot Heads, black and tan draft beers. The winery is standing room only, crowded with happy people enjoying the local music trio.

"Hare Finnish called me!" Cashel shouts over the music. "He's doing a big rogaining expedition starting right in our backyard."

"No way," Cutter says. "Where, man?"

"Ten national parks over twenty-one days starting at Glacier. The rest is top secret."

"What's rogaining besides the stuff you need for your bald spot?" Camas asks.

Cashal feels the top of his head.

"They're ultra-endurance orienteering events," Reeve answers.

"Holy shit," Camas says, looking a little worried.

"Yeah, they aim to keep all racers out for the entire event," Cutter says.

Camas stuffs a large piece of pizza in her mouth.

"That's elegant, princess," Cashal says.

"This princess is in the carbo-load lane for the rogaine." Camas chair dances to the music.

CHAPTER 15
BERINGIA NATIONAL PARK, RUSSIA - 3,053,233 HA
(64.2200, -173.1800)

Thomas and Sarah walk reverently through Widener Library, holding hands. They wind playfully through the stacks as Thomas whispers a Percy Shelley poem.

"The fountains mingle with the river, and the rivers with the ocean, the winds of heaven mix forever, with a sweet emotion; nothing in the world is single; all things by a law divine, in one spirit meet and mingle. Why not I with thine?"

Sarah smiles, looks around. She takes a book from a shelf to appear less conspicuous as the lovely recipient of romantic poetry.

Thomas continues. "See the mountains kiss high heaven, and the waves clasp one another; no sister-flower would be forgiven, if it disdained its brother; and the sunlight clasps the earth, and the moonbeams kiss the sea: what is all this sweet work worth, if thou kiss not me?"

Sarah giggles. She leans in, and their lips meet softly.

They look up to see Olivier seated at a table in the far corner and make their way across the library.

"I've decided I will make this my life's best and last work," Olivier says.

"Don't say last, but that is excellent news!" Sarah says excitedly.

"Now, how will we do it?"

Thomas and Sarah look surprised.

"You came to me." Olivier reminds them. "Didn't you have it all figured out?"

"Parts of it," they answer in unison.

"Well, shoot." Olivier lifts his Visconti Watermark fountain pen over a yellow legal pad.

Thomas looks at Sarah. She nods for him to go ahead.

Thomas addresses Olivier with a confident tone. "Each state will have a jewel, a green park refuge icon. The people will be inspired by history and beauty thereupon. A web of national land treasures for all the world to see. Species saved, air and waters forever clean for grandchildren, you and me."

Olivier takes notes. "Nice rhyme and vision. The national parks will be the inspiration. What about the populace? What's going to get us over the three-quarters mark?"

Sarah is nervous. Thomas gives her a nudge.

"We provide clean air and water and safe, natural spaces to people of color," Sarah says boldly.

Olivier writes it down carefully. "What else?"

"We overlay the color green on a map over people of color in the United States and sponsor a Green Amendment Brain Trust conference. We'll invite the world's top green energy, environmental, and climate experts from academia, government, and private industry to develop the technology to repair and deliver clean air and water to those people and provide permanent protections to national parks and the surroundings. Then you figure out how to get the states to call a constitutional convention."

"Yes, that's one way to amend the Constitution, but

there's only been one -- the original 1787 Philadelphia convention. The problem is, the language in the current Constitution about how to implement a second one is dangerously
vague, and I worry that to open it up could let some vermin
creep in."

"That's when you figure out a way to limit it to just our
freedom to breathe clean air and drink clean water," Sarah
says sweetly.

Olivier nods. He looks Thomas and Sarah in the eye
without smiling. He takes a deep breath. "We need someone
to lead it."

"We have you," Sarah responds.

"No, we need a young, inspirational person of color."

"Thomas is young and black," Sarah offers.

"I always forget that," Olivier says. "You are an old soul,
young Thomas, and indeed an inspiration, but I think we
need a woman. Don't ask me why. Just a feeling I have."

Thomas and Sarah say in unison, "We have her."

CHAPTER 16

KAENG KRACHAN NATIONAL PARK, THAILAND – 291,400 HA

(12.9103, 99.6561)

Traveling via train, ferry, bicycle, electric bus, and on foot, Tilly spreads the *"One More Year. Keep your stuff, people."* message across the greenest countries of Europe.

Tilly hikes along a dramatic cliff above the Geiranger fjord in Norway. Two days later, Tilly walks past a *One More Year* digital billboard in an Oslo train station, *Ett år til. Behold tingene deres, folkens.* She runs through Frognerparken and stops to meditate among the bronze statues of people holding onto trees at the Gustav Vigeland fountain. She finds her way to join a large group of students listening to an environmental speech in the University of Oslo's plaza. A banner reading *Arne Naesse Institute of Deep Ecology* hangs behind the speaker.

Tilly rides on the Gornergrat train with views of the dramatic Matterhorn in Switzerland. She sits at a café within the Frau Gerolds Garten made up of converted shipping containers in Zurich's bohemian area. A rotating back-lit illuminated pillar of a *One More Year* billboard on the street announces *Noch ein Jahr. Behalte eure Sachen, Leute.* Tilly joins a climate protest in downtown Zurich, marching with a group of young people as she carries a *There is no Planet B* sign.

Tilly is at Picadilly Circus, London, wearing an Extinction Rebellion T-shirt. She stands in front of the Shaftesbury Memorial Fountain of the winged god Anteros with the founder of Extinction Rebellion, Gail Bradbrook, speaking to a group of several hundred people for the unveiling of the *One More Year* electronic billboard.

Dark figures emerge, running through the misty fog under the Dark Hedges' twisted birch tree tunnel. As the ominous-looking herd approaches, the condensation of their breath floats into the air as they sing the Game of Thrones theme. Their voices rise in dramatic melody, then break into joyous laughter. A handful of the young Belfast runners and Tilly wear jerseys that read *I'm not afraid of the White Walkers (fossil fuel)*. One runner wears a *Love Leitum - ban fracking!* t-shirt.

Tilly runs through Paris with the Eiffel Tower in view, wearing a *Pour un Climat de Paix* T-shirt. She walks to board a train and a *One More Year* digital billboard is on the station wall, *Une année supplémentaire. Garde tes affaires plus longtemps, les gens.*

Tilly cycles around a picturesque Portuguese medieval village and up a hill to the Castle of Marvão. The next day in Lisbon, she unveils the digital billboard in the Praca do Rossio to a cheering crowd. *Mais um ano. Mantenha suas coisas por mais tempo, pessoal.* Tilly holds up her phone to show Liam and her curly black-haired dog Pedro, affectionately known as P, the Portuguese Water Dogs in the crowd.

GUIANA AMAZONIAN PARK, FRENCH GUIANA – 2,030,000 HA

(2.6358, -53.5913)

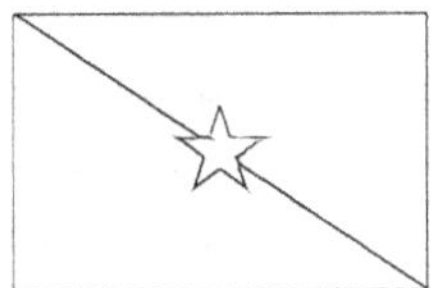

Camas sits with Josh at Heaven's Brother's café. She answers her phone. "How's it going?!"

"It's great! I'm in P's ancestors' land, and I've seen a few Porties. I miss him. How's he doing?"

"You miss P more than your best friend and husband?"

Tilly laughs. "You know that's not true. I do wish you were here. You always get to the heart of the matter."

"I am heart, sista."

"Yes, you are."

"You're getting loads of good press. Guess what?!"

"I can't guess."

"I got invited to do an adventure expedition, and I also have a money-making idea for One More Year."

"Wow! Tell me about the expedition first."

"Reeve invited me to be on a team with Cutter. There's one more guy who's a blowhard with an accent, but supposedly he's one of the best there is in the sport."

"That sounds right up your alley. You love orienteering and running. What does Josh think about all of it?"

"He seems OK. Sometimes it's hard to get him to talk about his feelings."

"Sounds like someone else I know."

"Me? I talk about my feelings all the time. Like just yesterday, I told Josh I love beer and pizza."

"Funny. And what's the other thing, the money-making idea?"

"It's a board game for One More Year."

"Hmmm… and why are we doing a board game?"

"It's an environmental board game. I don't have a name for it yet, but it's just like my favorite game, Risk, but instead of capturing, maiming, and killing hundreds of thousands of people to conquer the world, you save them, and the animals… and the air and the ocean."

"It sounds awesome. We can always use more money for the cause."

"It'll give me another reason to shake my moneymaker."

Tilly laughs. "I'm sure! Tell Graeme about it. I think his Uncle Bill came from the old school board game biz."

"Thanks for the tip! We can draw it up when you're back Saturday."

"Listen, Cam. I won't be home for a few more weeks."

"What?! You and Liam are newlyweds, and I need you back here for One More Year!"

"I haven't told Liam yet, so don't tell him, please. I've added some countries to the One More Year tour."

"We won't be able to get the billboards set up in time. Just come home, and you can go back."

"They haven't asked for a billboard, and that's too wasteful in fuel to come back. Who knows if I'll ever be back here."

"Where are you going?"

"Oh…" Tilly pauses, then sputters, "just Asia and Africa."

"Well, that certainly helps me send out the rescue team.

Just head over to that continent in the Southern Hemisphere, just past South America."

"OK, Southern Asia and West Africa."

"Tilly. Where?"

"Sierra Leone, Liberia, Cote d'Ivoire, Afghanistan, and Myanmar."

"What the fuck? Are you joking? Liberia. That's where Goddafi ruled!"

"That's Libya, not Liberia, although he had connections to Liberia. And, no, I'm not joking."

"And there's war in Afghanistan! I knew I shouldn't have left you. Those countries are dangerous!"

"I promise I won't go to war zones."

"And what about Ebola?!"

"Ebola is under control."

"You are *not* traveling there!"

"I am, Camas, and I need your help."

"With what?"

"Contacting the environmental ministers in each of those Neen countries."

"Why would I? And what the hell is Neen?"

"Because you're CFO of One More Year and my best friend? Neen is non-green. I got tired of writing and saying the latter."

"It's only one more syllable. You've lost your mind! I'm flying there to get you!"

CHAPTER 18

FIORDLAND NATIONAL PARK, NEW ZEALAND – 1,200,000 HA

(-45.4156, 167.7167)

"I have an extra mask if you'd like it," Durga offers to Pittsburgh mayor Evangeline Forest as they walk along the Monongahela River in Clairton, Pennsylvania, just outside of Pittsburgh.

"Thanks, it is especially rank today."

"Thanks for meeting with me, Mayor. I'm headed to Washington DC next week to see my daughter. She gets upset with me for not listening to her. She is so smart, and I don't know why I make her so frustrated. I thought if I see her in person, it might help," Durga says.

"I think that's part of the mother-daughter dynamic, at least until she's older. My daughter's in her thirties now, and we're finally able to talk without me thoroughly disgusting her."

"That's good news. Thank you. Now, tell me the bad news about Clairton. It's a bit of an ironic name. Clean-air... Clairton."

"True. In the mid-2000s, they reported this community to have the highest cancer risk rates from air pollutants in the nation. Pittsburgh is the eighth-worst city for year-round particle pollution.

"It's steel production here, right?"

"And fracking too. And now there's a massive, $6 billion ethane cracker being built thirty miles northwest of Pittsburgh, expected to emit 2.2 million tons of greenhouse gases annually. In other words, all of Pittsburgh's work on combatting climate change through 2030 will be negated by a single plant. Clairton is an example of a fence-line community. People are getting fed up with being told to be a good turtle and go back into their shells until they can breathe again."

"One study reported that people of color in the northeast and mid-Atlantic are living with sixty-six percent more air pollution. We think the number is higher when you add coal and natural gas plants, which are usually near disadvantaged communities," Durga adds.

"Exactly. The American Lung Association's recent State of the Air report said that 74 million people of color live in counties that received at least one failing grade for ozone or particle pollution, and over 14 million people of color live in counties that received failing grades on all three measures."

"Shit."

"And then there's climate pounding down on us. Some reports make it sound like the climate is making things worse for cities' and counties' attempts to have cleaner air. That's an even bigger irony since the pollution itself has impacted the climate. Now it feels like we can't catch up. I'm sure you heard that Forty-Five rolled back regulations that reduced potent greenhouse methane from oil and gas wells this summer. Let's just throw that fireball in the mix, shall we?!" Evangeline says passionately.

"That's why we need the green amendment in all the states, not just here in Pennsylvania. So these blasted rollbacks can't happen with each change in political adminis-tration!"

"Preachin' to the choir."

"Hallelujah."

"Hi, my love."

"Camas called you, didn't she?" Tilly says to Liam on the phone. She sits at the quaint Quase Café in Lisbon's Alfama neighborhood with a plate of fluffy mini pancakes.

"She did. I miss you."

"I miss you too and love you."

"I'm worried about your plans."

"I'm just going to the Fado museum today."

"Not funny. I'll fly to join you."

"No, you need to stay with P and help your dad after his surgery."

"You can't travel to those places alone."

"Of course I can."

"It would be much better with a travel buddy."

"I'll be fine. Give P a hug and tell him I'm in his home-land, Portugal. It's really special. I wish you both were here with me."

"We will be someday. Maybe we'll move there."

"Maybe! Sweet dreams. I'll call you tomorrow to give you my details."

"I don't like it but it sounds like you've made your mind up."

"I have."

"Oh, I almost forgot. Sarah Montana called and said she's been trying to get a hold of you. She said it's important."

"OK, thanks. I'll call her. I love you."

"I love you too."

Tilly runs along the Tagus river in the Belem District of Lisbon with colorfully painted buildings with clay tile roofs lining the shore. She answers her phone, still running. "Liam called you."

Anika James, a beautiful, tall black Belgian woman with an Amazonian athletic build, is on her bike trainer spinning, talking hands-free on her cell phone attached to the bike.

"Yes, he did. How are you, lovely? I miss you. I can't believe you've been in Europe and haven't come to see me."

"I miss you too. I'm sorry. Camas booked this tour for the One More Year billboards, and it's been a whirlwind."

"That's why I should come on the rest of your tour. To spend time with you and keep you safe."

"Do you think a six-foot-five supermodel triathlete will help me blend into the crowd?"

"You missed black and French-speaking."

"Beautiful black French-speaking six-foot-five supermodel triathlete."

Anika laughs.

"Anika, I so want to see you, but I need to go to these places on my own. I'm taking a freighter home from Shanghai. Why don't you meet me there before I head home?"

"The French and my skin color could come in handy in Cote d'Ivoire."

"I'll be fine. Really."

"Well, I guess at least I could tell Camas and Liam that I put you safely on the boat home. I'll come to China. Send me the date. Please be careful. Love you."

"Love you too."

CHAPTER 19
SØR-SPITSBERGEN NATIONAL
PARK, NORWAY – 8,504,000 HA

(77.2626, 16.0738)

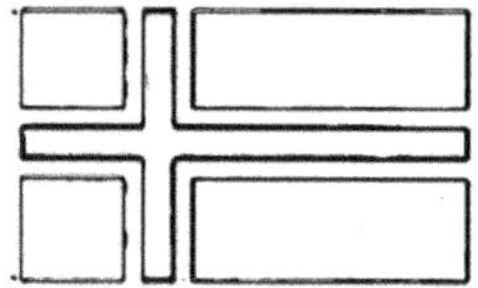

J osh and Camas make dinner together in their cottage's tiny kitchen with vintage tile and Fiesta ware.

"OK, the stew's on the stove. Let's play strip rogaine!" Camas calls.

"How'd you hear about this again?" Josh asks.

"I was online researching rogaining and found it. They have metro-gaine, paddle-gaine, moto-gaine, paddle-gaine, and snow-gaine. "

"What are the rules?'

"We each have something on our list to find, and whoever finds it first gets to make a request of the other."

Josh laughs. "Are there rules around the requests?"

Camas looks at her phone, "Let me see. Oh yeah, the official rules say no animals, weapons, or drug enhancements."

"Whew!" Josh exaggerates.

"The request can be to remove an article of clothing, or to kiss any part of the body above the sternum including the arms and hands, or perform a dance, or recite a requested phrase not to include vulgarity or profanity."

"Seems like good clean fun."

Camas continues reading, "...until such time as one player is naked and then all bets are off!"

"Hah! You made that up!"

"Maybe," Camas teases.

The two grab their compasses and their lists.

Camas's list says *find a kitchen tool that has can whip*. Camas finds a vintage whisk with a red handle in a canister on top of the stove. Josh takes off his beanie.

Josh's list reads *find a tasty alcoholic beverage not in the refrigerator*. Josh finds a crowler of MatchLove Brewery's Hazy Milkshake IPA in Camas's backpack in the garage. Camas takes off her shirt, revealing a teal bra with bright pink peonies.

Camas's list reads *find a tool smaller than a breadbox and bigger than a pocket knife*. Camas finds a bicycle wrench set in Josh's mountain bike under-seat saddlebag. Josh takes off a sock.

Josh's list reads *find a tool not in your own toolbox that has a spring*. Josh finds an eyelash curler in the back of the bathroom closet in Camas's makeup bag. Camas takes off her ponytail holder, her strawberry blonde curls falling over her lightly freckled cheeks.

Camas and Josh sit in their underwear at the small dining room table, eating stew and drinking a bottle of Lake Bijou Nez red wine.

Josh kisses Camas. "Hey, I was on the iMac and saw a text from Cashal that said to call him. Something about a video from the race you need to watch and something about going on a diet, so your ass isn't so fat."

"You read my text?"

"It popped up."

"Oh, OK. Speaking of asses. That guy is one. A misogynistic ass to boot. I hope I can tolerate him during the race."

"You will. You have a beautiful ass, by the way," he says, leaning his head over and bending down to look at her fanny in her underwear.

"Thank you," Camas smiles, "Hey, how was your ride with Ike and Joe?"

"Fast and fun. Since Reeve and Cutter were tied up training with their compasses, we invited a girl we met at Heaven's Brothers to join us. She turned out to be skilled."

Camas gulps her red wine. She is quiet. She stands up and starts washing dishes.

"Cam, are you OK?"

"Why couldn't you find another guy to ride with?" she says, still staring at the dishes.

Josh stands up and walks up close behind her. He puts his arms around the front of her and his head alongside hers. He speaks softly. "Hey, you're about to take off for three weeks on the fantastical foot, flight, and fluvial whatchamajigger race with three dudes, and I trust you. Is it OK that I trust you?"

Camas turns around to him. She looks up into his eyes. "Yes. I'm happy you trust me."

"OK, then. Do you think you can trust me too? I only want to be strip rogaining and any other kind of gainin' with you."

Camas smiles. They kiss deeply. She takes his hand and leads him toward the bedroom.

"Hey, is this in the rulebook?"

Camas pretends to read from an invisible phone in her hand and says in a mock official voice, "National Associations may adjust the rules for specific events where appropriate."

"Boom," Josh says as he closes the door behind them.

CHAPTER 20
SHEY PHOKSUNDO NATIONAL PARK, NEPAL – 355,500 HA

(29.5026, 82.8210)

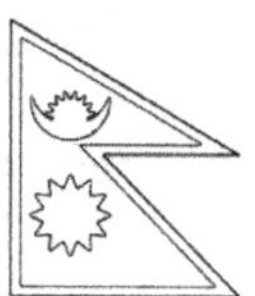

"Good morning, Till. Oh, it's the middle of the night, isn't it?"

"No, just evening, sweetie. I was just about to call you."

"I know you said you'd call, but I couldn't wait. I'm worried."

"Thanks for calling, my love."

"What's the itinerary? I want every hotel and contact, please."

"Camas will give you the contacts. I'm taking a freighter from Lisbon to Namibia the day after tomorrow. It'll take twenty-one days."

"Camas is pretty involved in her race training."

"I know she's busy. It's great. But she did put the Neen country itinerary together for me."

"Neen?"

"The non-green countries."

"Got it. Is your goal to green them?" Liam asks.

"I wouldn't presume that. I just want to observe."

"Promise me we'll travel together in the future."

"I promise."

"And Till, please be safe."

Tilly stands at the edge of a cement pier at the industrial Port of Lisboa with gargantuan cargo ships topped with stacks of colorful shipping containers towering behind her. Her rolling backpack rests on the ground.

"Tilly! Thanks for calling me," Sarah says, walking down the Spanish Steps in the Dupont Circle neighborhood of DC. She holds Thomas's hand.

"No problem. I'm just about to get on a ship to Africa. What's up?"

"Wow. I want to know more, but I know you're rushed."

"Remember Thomas Foolerin?"

"Of course. He tried to help us get the green amendment in time to stop the Copper Cobra mine. He's outstanding. A rhyming prince."

"I think so too," Sarah says, smiling at Thomas. Well, he's still at it, and we've teamed up with a couple of people, but we need your help."

"What is it?"

"We want to bring attention to bringing clean air and water to people of color."

"That's an admirable goal."

"We believe that if we can shine a light on the lack thereof, we can create a movement big enough to get a green amendment to the U.S. constitution."

"It couldn't get traction before."

"I know. That's why I'm calling you. You're a woman of color. You've created movements."

"I never created them by myself."

"I know. I just thought you might have some insights and ideas for us."

"Who's on the team you mentioned?"

"An old guy who's a constitutional legal guru, my mom who has been working closely with the states trying to get amendments to their constitutions individually, my boss, Senator Mesapologic, Thomas and..." she takes a deep breath, "hopefully you."

Tilly laughs. "I'm on the other side of the planet, but count me in! You can count Camas in too."

"Oh, Tilly! Thank you!!"

"Sarah, I have a long boat ride. Let me give this some thought. I'll talk to Camas, and I'll be in touch."

"Great! It's so good to hear your voice."

"Yours too. Talk soon, Sarah."

"Travel safely!"

"She said yes!" Sarah stops to kiss Thomas on the steps.

CHAPTER 21

GAMBELLA NATIONAL PARK, ETHIOPIA – 501,600 HA

(8.0046, 34.0641)

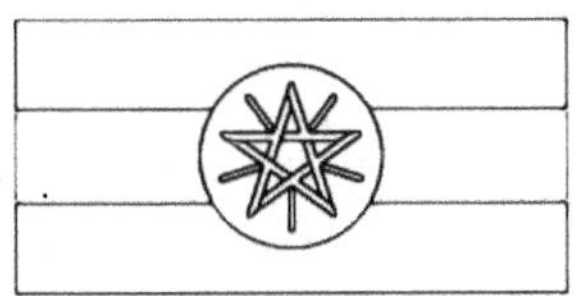

Reeve, Cashal, Cutter, and Camas sit around a screen in Reeve's bike shop. They each have a glass of beer in hand, and a few post-training empties are scattered on the bicycle workbench.

"Seems they liked our team video despite Camas's sappy answers about saving the world and that we all came together to learn more about ourselves. It must have been your brògan mòra," Cashal says, looking down at Camas's cleavage, which appears lovely as usual above the zipper pull of her snug One More Year mountain bike jacket.

"I agree it's a miracle since all you did was rattle off a list of obscure race titles from the nerdy Hogwarts School of Compass Mastery."

"Smarter is faster," Cashal responds.

"Respect. They must have liked your braggart brogue, brother," Cutter says.

Reeve quickly changes the subject. "The instructions for the video say we're supposed to watch this together and with no one else around." He taps his laptop to start the video.

Hare Finnish appears on the screen, sitting at a desk with

shelves behind him full of books, vintage explorer gear, and framed color and black and white photo adventure scenes of climbers, kayakers, horseback riders, and skydivers.

"Welcome adventurers! Congratulations on receiving a ticket to race in some of the most spectacular playgrounds in the world -- ten national parks in Montana, Wyoming, Utah, Colorado, New Mexico, and Arizona. Please note that this video is for your eyes only. If it's discovered that you have shared it with anyone else, even your close family, you'll be disqualified at best and sued at worst. My slimy lawyer made me say that last part, but I think it's probably true."

Camas raises her eyes to the guys. "It's like Willy Wonka meeting the golden ticket holders," she says excitedly.

"Shhhhh!" Cashal shushes grumpily.

"When you signed on the dotted line releasing us of all liability upon injury or death, you also signed a confidentiality clause. It's important that the locations are kept secret even after the start of the race for your safety but mainly for promotion and ratings. If one of you dies, that will be hard to keep a secret, so stay alive, will you?"

Camas turns to Reeve with a worried look.

"You'll be issued a set number of supplies and tools at the start of each segment, and, besides the standard racing gear, we emailed a list of your mandatory equipment..."

Cashal gives Camas a smirk.

"...including a wetsuit, fins and mask, crampons, climbing gear, and motorbike pannier."

Reeve, Cutter, and Cashal are surprised.

"Don't get excited that you can bring more stuff since you'll have a motorbike. They're just for getting from one park to the next. The bikes will need to cross some rugged terrain, and I advise you to go as light as possible. Most of all, stay healthy and rested before race day. You'll need all the energy, strength, and stamina you can muster for the twenty-one-day expedition. Let's take a look at where you'll be racing."

Cashal ends the video.

"It's so exciting! What's our team name?" Camas asks.

"Who gives a fuck about the name? Can you climb and swim?" Cashal says.

"Yes, I can. Don't be a party pooper. How about Camas's Cuties? You're not cute, Cashal, but our cuteness will zero you out."

Cutter and Reeve laugh.

"You're all redheads. How about the Glacier Gingers?" Reeve suggests.

"I like it," Cutter nods.

"Sounds weak, man," Cashal grunts.

"Fits you, then," Camas teases, punching Cashal's shoulder.

"Blueys is an Aussie term for gingers. How about the Bastard Blueys?" Cashal suggests.

"Brave Blueys?" Reeve offers.

"Yes!" Camas shouts, raising her hands in the air.

"Does that mean I need to dye my hair?" Reeve jokes.

Reeve and Cutter laugh. Cashal shakes his head and takes a swig of beer.

"Hey, Till. I'm going underground for three weeks. I don't know how I'll get through without you. We can't have any technology except for a one-channel satellite phone for emergency calls out to the race staff."

"I love it," Tilly says, talking to Camas on her phone from a small, barebones cargo ship cabin.

"What?! You're not going to miss me?"

"Of course, I am, silly. I already miss you, but I love the no-technology part of your race. We all could use a month with no technology."

"You'll bring the economy to a halt."

"You don't believe that."

"You're right. I don't. People would send smoke signal tweets and send a boat up the river to buy shit."

"That's sad, not funny. You leave tomorrow morning. Are you nervous?"

"We got the race route. It sounds brutal."

"What's the route?"

"Our line might be tapped. They made us sign a non-disclosure. It's top secret."

"OK."

"Aren't you going to ask me what it is?"

"You just told me it's hush-hush."

"You're no fun. You're supposed to try to find out."

Tilly laughs. Feigning curiosity, "Cam, pleeeeeease. I won't tell a soul."

"I don't know. I could get in big trouble."

"I'm your best friend. I'm on a cargo ship on the Atlantic. Your secret's safe with me," Tilly says dramatically, smiling.

Camas whispers, "10 national parks. Canyonlands, Chaco, Dinosaur, Glacier, Grand Canyon, Grand Teton, Great Sand Dunes, Hovenweep, Mesa Verde, and Rocky Mountain."

"Wow! Those are the parks the National Park Service reported were the most threatened by oil and gas mining."

"No shit?"

"Remember, I read that to you over coffee at Heaven's Brothers."

"I must not have been listening."

"You did have your headphones in. The organizer must have chosen those on purpose."

"Huh? The organizer is a Hollywood Crocodile Dundee. I don't think he's a green head."

"It could hardly be a coincidence."

"Threatened or not, the parks are going to break our asses."

"Please be careful. It's your first race, and I want you back safe and sound because you're my best friend and because I signed us up for a new project."

"Uh oh."

"You know Sarah, the anti-plastic champion."

"Yep. Refill, Bill!"

"She's working so people of color can have fresh air and clean water."

"Hey, I want that too!" Camas jokes.

"We all want it, right?"

"What can I do?"

"You just focus on your race and have fun, but I just thought that when you need to get your mind off of the excruciating pain on mile 243 in the middle of a desert..."

"Don't remind me."

"...you might give her cause some thought."

"OK, sista, will do."

"And, forget you told me about the route, OK? That info might help Sarah, and if I share it, I don't want you to get in trouble."

"Got it. If I can't figure out how to send you a smoke signal somehow, I'll see you on the flip side. Be safe in those crazy countries. You know, this will be the longest we've ever been apart since we met," Camas says softly.

"I know. Don't get disqualified trying to call me. You, please be safe too. Love you, Cam."

"Love you too, Till."

"The network just called, and they want us to produce the race live," Fremont says, his weary face stressed as he drives along the Malibu coastline with the top down on his custom convertible Tesla.

"Why is that?" Hare asks, running along a trail with Felice.

"Something about needing to fill an earlier slot and that it'll be cheaper."

"Bring it on."

CHAPTER 22

SANJIANGYUAN NATIONAL NATURE RESERVE, CHINA – 36,300,000 HA

(34.0055, 96.2040)

Cutter drives his orange 1979 International Harvester Scout on Highway 2 towards Glacier National Park. Reeve is in the passenger seat. Camas and Cashal ride in the back.

"I'm surprised your boyfriend let you do this race with us," Cashal says. "I wouldn't have."

"Why is it any different from Reeve going when he's married to his wife back in Sandglass?" Camas asks, annoyed.

"Camas and Josh have a great relationship," Reeve says.

"Because men are different. They've always been able to travel anywhere regardless of a woman," Cashal says.

"That sounds like a sexist pile of crap," Camas responds.

"You wait. You're not going to be able to control yourself when you spend time with this sexy Scotsman, and your relationship will go to hell."

"Don't hold your breath."

Reeve and Cutter look at each other and raise their eyebrows.

"What does your wife think about you racing with Camas, Reeve," Cutter asks.

"She knows we're close friends, and she's friends with Camas too," Reeve says. "We've always lived by the fly-on-the-wall guideline that if our best friend walked in the room when our partner was talking with a person of the opposite sex, the friend wouldn't feel uncomfortable."

"What does Josh think?"

"That it's fine. He's happy if I'm happy. I kind of wish he'd care more," Camas says as she looks out the window.

Tilly's husband, Liam, a handsome, athletic young man with short curly hair and sparkling blue eyes, sits with Josh and his father partner, Liz, at a table on the island cottage patio overlooking Lake Bijou Nez. Grilled vegetables and salmon, freshly baked bread, farmer's market greens with huckleberries and local blue cheese, wine, and fresh flowers fill the table. Graeme, ruggedly handsome with short grey-blonde hair, walks up to the table with beer for Josh and Liam as the sun sets over the lake.

"Thank's for inviting me to your island," Josh says. "This is delicious."

"We're happy you're spending the night, Josh," Liz says warmly, a few strands of grey sparkling in her shoulder-length auburn hair under the amber sunset.

"Yeah, man. You'll be christening the new guest cottage," Liam agrees.

"The guest cottage is bigger than this cottage," Graeme laughs.

"We thought it would be nice to have it for times like this so people can visit the island and not have to rush back."

"I saw it. It's so great. Nice work, Liam."

"Thanks. I had to do something when I was missing Tilly

so much. Also, Dad is having an operation, and I'll be out here helping Liz with the old geezer."

"What's the operation, Mr. Selkirk, if you don't mind me asking?"

"I'm finally getting a second surgery on my leg. It's an old cycling injury."

"I'm sure you'll have a fast recovery."

"Thanks, Josh."

Josh looks out over the lake. "I know the feeling of missing someone. My gal is out being her rugged, sporty self with three guys. Do you ever worry about Tilly and other men?"

"I did for a time, after our first wedding attempt and she was off biking across the country."

"I bet."

Liz puts her hand on Graeme's knee under the table.

"But I told myself there was nothing I could do if something did happen. All I could do is be trustworthy myself. To offer that part of my character to show I love her. Damn. That sounds corny, doesn't it?"

"I think corny gets the girl, man. Camas is super jealous. And sometimes she tells me things about other guys, and when I don't respond and act jealous myself, she thinks I don't care."

"O, beware, my lord, of jealousy; It is the green-ey'd monster..." Graeme says.

"Have you talked with her about it?" Liz asks gently.

"I haven't. I just don't react. The Thirteenth Amendment abolished involuntary servitude. We don't own each other even though we are in a committed partnership. I've never been a jealous person before, so it's hard for me to understand her."

"Even though it may sound silly, a woman can interpret no reaction as not caring," Liz says gently.

"I need to pretend to be jealous?"

"No, of course not, but y...."

Graeme interrupts, "May I?"

"Go ahead," Liz nods.

"If you stake your claim in a 21st-century manner, it can go a long way to steady the boat."

"Dad, get to the point," Liam says.

"Who sang, if you liked it, you should have put a ring on it?" Graeme asks.

"Beyonce," Josh answers. "I don't think I would tie the knot to curb jealousy."

"No, but if you've already decided to leap, it could be a nice bonus."

"I can see that," Josh says.

Liam holds his glass up. The four bring their glasses together and the sweet chime floats over the mock-orange syringa hillside to the lake's shore.

CHAPTER 23
GABAL ELBA NATIONAL PARK,
EGYPT – 3,560,000 HA

(22.2000, 36.3333)

Tilly writes with a precise and flowing hand. As though softening a porcupine quill for weaving, she puts the end tip of her pen in her mouth, closes her eyes, then opens them as she writes the name of each national park with a silent prayer.

Dear Sarah,

The Parklands Enviro-Climate Challenge is about to announce its race locations. These will be well-televised events with images of some of the most beautiful natural places in the United States. Stage peaceful protests at each park as the racers come through. Each park has environmental degradation challenges. Find the shadow – air pollution, water contamination, cultural destruction -- and shine a light. Concurrently, organize urban demonstrations in communities with people of color living in the most severe pollution.

Camas is off the grid racing, but I will assemble One More Year, Petal Pedal Ride, and Raise it Red influencers to spread the word. Call Reina McCaring at the EPA if you need help from the inside.

I wish I were there to help more. Be safe and do good work!

Your friend in peaceful love of the planet,

Tilly

Canyonlands National Park, Utah
Chaco Culture National Historical Park, New Mexico
Dinosaur National Monument, Colorado and Utah
Glacier National Park, Montana
Grand Canyon National Park, Arizona
Grand Teton National Park, Wyoming
Great Sand Dunes National Park, Colorado
Hovenweep National Monument, Colorado and Utah
Mesa Verde National Park, Colorado
Rocky Mountain National Park, Colorado

Tilly takes a photo of the letter. She walks from her cabin up to a railing on the ship's deck, taps her phone, and emails the letter to Sarah. Tilly scrolls slowly through photos of Liam and Pedro, then looks out over the expanse of the Atlantic Ocean.

CHAPTER 24

KERAMA SHOTŌ NATIONAL PARK, JAPAN - 3,520 HA

(26.2020, 127.3574)

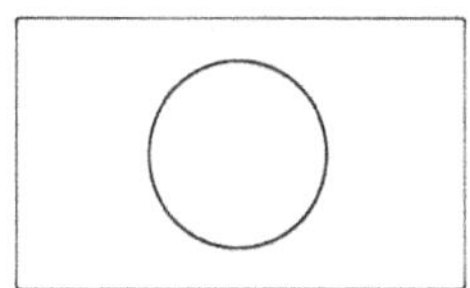

Camas paces back and forth in front of her race pack. She walks over to Reeve, Cutter, and Cashal, finishing filling their packs and dressing at the racers' staging area at Glacier National Park.

"We need to be at the river stage in 20 minutes. Get your shit together, guys!" Camas calls out.

"Got it, Cam," Cutter says.

"No problem," Reeve answers.

Cashal's shirtless fair-skinned back is turned to Camas. He doesn't answer. She walks up as he puts white tape on his nipples.

"Hey, sissy, what are the pasties on your chebs?" Camas asks.

"For chafing. Didn't you catch that in the seminar, blondie? Would you like me to do yours?"

Camas looks down at her chest and walks off.

Teams from twenty-eight states and twenty-two countries stand in a grassy meadow next to the Apgar Amphitheater on the shore of Lake MacDonald. The energy is palpable as the athletes employ warm-up and relaxation tactics for their nerves.

Camas chews gum and dances with headphones as athletes from other teams look at her curiously. Her face is tense. A few athletes smile and join in with some international dance moves. Cashal stretches at the edge of the group with a severe expression. The teams wear matching jerseys with patches identifying their country of origin. The Brave Blueys wear navy blue and dark aqua shirts, and jackets with orange accents. Brave Bluey and U.S. flag patches adorn the sleeves. Reeve wears an orange knit cap to match his teammates' ginger-colored hair.

The chop-chop sounds of a helicopter are heard in the distance. Hare and a strong television cameraman lean off the side, filming the athletes below.

"It's a stellar group of athletes down there! We're just a few minutes from the start of the Parklands Enviro-Climate Challenge!" Hare shouts into the camera. "Fifty international teams are vying for the coveted first place and prize money. At the top of the list is the strong, experienced New Zealand Team, the Blenheim Blizzards. The Silicon Squalls from Silicon Valley, California, are no strangers to racing. Other than their compasses, they left their high-tech gadgets at home. All four Spanish athletes have won important adventure race titles, so the Toro Tornadoes are here to win big. One of the best adventure racers on the planet, Scottish athlete Cashal Threinfhir is racing with three Yanks on the Brave Blueys team. No one quite understands his team, including one newbie female athlete, but we are here to see what they can do!"

The athletes cheer from below.

Hare continues his commentary for the helicopter cameraman. "As tough as the rugged coast of Brittany from which they hail, the Bretagne Badgers join the elite group. Other teams expected to compete at the highest level are the Queensland Compasses, the Supercell Swedes, the Danish Derechos, the Tasmanian Thunders, the Missouri Climatrons, the Italo Icebergs, the Tokyo Tsunamis, the Denver Dustdevils, the Hawaiian Heatwaves, the Brazilian Blowouts, the Canadian Cyclones, the Welsch Wildfires, and the Hamburg Hailstones."

The helicopter makes its descent to the pad below.

"Of course, there are thirty-three more teams that have shown up today to make their mark in the greatest race on the planet. We'll be watching them closely because there always seems to be an upset or two or ten in these races!"

The helicopter blades chop loudly just above the crowd of athletes and spectators.

Cashal calls out. "Quit that dancing and listen up!"

"I'm trying to calm myself."

The Blueys huddle up to him.

"We haven't even started, and you need a breath mint," Camas grimaces.

"Garlic contains allicin which stimulates circulation and blood flow to sexual organs in both men and women," Cashal says.

"I think your brain needs blood flow, not your dick."

"Hey, Blueys, let's listen to Captain Cashal," Reeve says, buckling his pack.

"Thanks, buddy." He clears his throat. "We're about to get a major stick up our asses in the form of Hare's cheers, the cameras, and adrenaline."

"And your garlic ass-a-line," Camas jokes.

Cashal ignores her. "So, if we want to win, we need to

have energy for the whole race, not blow our wad on the start."

"That's no fun. If we're in the lead, we'll more likely get on TV!" Camas says. "Hare likes fast."

"Cashal's right," Cutter agrees.

"Hare got his name for running too many adventure races in the lead and then getting overtaken at the end. He never could figure it out," Cashal says.

"Oh yeah. Tortoise and the *hare*. How'd he get to be a big adventure race hero then?" Cutter asks.

"He's gorgeous with an accent," Camas says.

"I knew you thought I was sexy," Cashal says.

"Not," Camas turns away and looks up at the helicopter overhead.

"He was Special Air Service in the Aussie Army," Reeve says.

The helicopter lands on a pad near the athletes. Television cameras shoot at various angles. Hare jumps out of the chopper as the athletes cheer. A cameraman exits the helicopter.

Fremont Fonear stands on the edge of the amphitheater stage. Hare runs and jumps up onto the stage, then shakes Fremont's hand.

Hare turns to the athletes. "Are you ready?!"

The crowd roars. Fremont pulls a rope to lift a cloth cover from a giant billboard at the back of the stage. The board has a map of the United States with the words *Parklands Enviro-Climate Challenge* and red dots marking ten locations west of the Mississippi.

"In minutes, you'll begin the world's longest and most challenging adventure expedition."

The group of two hundred athletes, spectators, park rangers, race managers and support staff cheer.

"You'll race 760 miles through six states over twenty-one

days. Some of the challenges have never been achieved in an adventure expedition, and besides control points in each park, you'll have medallions to retrieve in five of the parks. Your captain will have the satellite phone. Per the rules you've signed, the phone can only be used to call race support. Any other communications will disqualify you and your team. It will track you for the fans, however. You're starting here at the magnificent Glacier National Park in Montana, known as the crown of the nation. We'll be telling viewers more about each of the parks as you race, but you'll roam with the ghosts of dinosaurs at Dinosaur National Monument and think you're in the Sahara Desert as you race through the tallest dunes in North American at the Great Sand Dunes. All in all, with the miles between the parks, you'll travel a total of 2,950 miles!"

The crowd cheers.

"OK, now for your surprise."

The crowd quiets.

"This race is Score-O!"

The athletes are surprised.

"You'll start here in Glacier, follow a set route of parks, and end in the magnificent Grand Canyon, but within the parks, the control points and medallions may be achieved in any order."

The crowd noise is a low hum of nervous mumbles.

"Yes, it's a huge game of strategy. We're giving your captains the details on getting from park to park as the race proceeds so you can strategize and make decisions about your route inside the parks."

There is chatter among the racers.

"Listen up! Here's your first segment! At the sound of the bell, you'll get your wetsuits and swim ten miles across Lake MacDonald. You'll have one kayak per team and are allowed to rest one at a time, but at least three of you must be in the water at all times. You'll navigate to your first control point. From there, you'll cycle up 1,900 feet and 39 miles over the Continental Divide at Logan Pass on the Going to the Sun Road. The bell will sound the start. Can I get a cheer? Parklands Enviro-Climate Challenge cheer?! One...two...three!"

The athletes and crowd roar, "Parklands Enviro-Climate Challenge!!"

The bell sounds, and the athletes run to put on their wetsuits.

"Wait, we need to break!" Camas shouts.

Cashal rolls his eyes. The four face each other and stack their hands in the center.

Hare notices that all the teams have left except the Blueys. He speaks into the camera, "Looks like the Blueys have held back for some team spirit."

"Brave Blueys on three," Camas shouts. "One, two..."

"Brave Blueys!!" they shout in unison as they raise their hands to the sky.

"Gie it laldy!" Cashal shouts.

CHAPTER 25
NIJHUM DWIP NATIONAL PARK,
BANGLADESH – 16,352 HA

(22.0937, 91.0072)

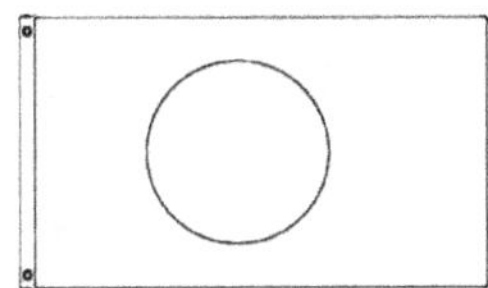

As the teams scramble to start the swim across Lake MacDonald, Hare and Fremont climb into the helicopter.

"You didn't tell me these parks are all on the edge of big mining projects," Fremont says over the headsets.

"A minor detail," Hare responds.

"Not too small to our sponsors, who are getting calls from oil and gas investors."

"Well, maybe these Yanks can't get climate change right on their own."

"Not sure how a bunch of endurance lunatics is going to help."

"We used to have passion like those lunatics," Hare says, looking down below.

"Mom, this is Thomas."

"So nice to meet you, Mrs. Gelderland," Thomas says, extending his hand.

"Very nice to meet you, Thomas," Durga smiles warmly.

"What brings you to DC?" Thomas asks.

"Just Sarah. Well, not just. Sarah."

"Mom, it's a wonderful coincidence because we want to show you something."

"OK. What is it?"

Thomas pulls out a map with colored circles around several areas.

"Can you tell me what this is?" Sarah asks.

Durga looks at Sarah, then at the map. She reviews it for a minute. "The brown circles look like they are around the ten most polluted cities."

"Bingo."

Thomas looks impressed.

"Anything else?"

Durga examines the map. "I think the blue circles mark cities with the highest population of people of color."

"Wow. That's impressive. How did you know that?" Thomas asks.

"Well, my life's work is to make clean air and water an inalienable right. Well, it already is an inalienable right, but to anchor that truth in the law. In any case, I know where the air and water aren't clean in this country."

"But, the demographics?" Sarah asks.

"I see of the top fifteen cities with the highest percentage of people of color, eight are in the most polluted cities." She puts her finger on the map. "Here's L.A., for example, with about seventy percent people of color and in the top five of ozone and particulate pollution. Oh, and over here is Phoenix with forty-five percent people of color in the top ten of polluted cities." She looks up. "What's the map for?"

"Mom, I'm sure you know that these cities, among many other towns and areas, have pollution inequality."

"Of course."

"No one, white or black or any color, should breathe unhealthy air that gives you asthma or drink water that gives you cancer. But studies say that African Americans are exposed to about fifty-six percent more pollution than is caused by their consumption, and Hispanics sixty-three percent more."

"Meanwhile, whites breathe about seventeen percent less air pollution than they cause, earning a sadly named 'pollution advantage' and giving us pause," Thomas adds.

Durga gives Sarah a curious look.

"Thomas likes to rhyme." Sarah smiles.

"Oh."

"Thomas and I are going to organize groups to bring attention to the fossil fuel pollution around the ten parks in the Parkland Enviro-Climate Challenge. You don't watch TV, but it's a popular show hosted by a famous Australian adventurer. We need your help to organize people in the most polluted cities when we're protesting from the parks."

"I did hear about it when I was in Arizona. When does it start?"

"It started today."

"That's be an organizing feat."

"They race for twenty-one days."

"What's the goal?"

"A constitutional convention for the green amendment."

"Those metro areas only represent about twelve states."

"And the race is another six states," Thomas says.

"Assuming those states would even call a constitutional convention, how are you going to get the other thirty-plus states?"

"We have some social movement oomph from triathlete Tilly DeMontagne. Olivier Clan's working on the problem too, but we'll cross that bridge when we get to it," Sarah says.

"Sarah, that's more than a bridge. That's the Grand Canyon," Durga says with a worried look.

"Martin Luther King Jr. wrote, 'There is no tactical theory so neat that a revolutionary struggle for a share of power can be won merely by pressing a row of buttons,'" Thomas recites.

"Can we count you in, Mom?"

Durga is quiet. She stands up, snaps a photo of the map on the table, and hugs Sarah firmly. "Send me the list of parks and the target date." She shakes Thomas's hand. "Keep her safe, Thomas, the rafe."

CHAPTER 26

SIGATOKA SAND DUNES, FIJI –
650 HA

(-18.1416, 177.5074)

T*elevision graphic and Hare's voiceover: Parklands Enviro-Climate Challenge, Map of U.S. with a dot on all ten parks, Glacier National Park's dot emphasized.*

"Glacier National Park is known as the crown of the continent with its pristine forests, alpine meadows, rugged mountains, spectacular lakes, and over 700 miles of trails. The park's iconic feature is the Continental Divide at 6,646 feet elevation on the famous Going-to-the-Sun Road."

Reeve, Cutter, Cashal, and Camas cycle strongly up the five percent grade towards Logan Pass through exquisite Glacier National Park.

"Your ass looks nice in the hot pink Spanx," Cashal says, riding close behind Camas.

"I'm glad it's appealing to you since I expect to be pulling your weak ass the last half of this adventure. You're the captain and already in the rear."

"I'm a rear man."

"I told you to knock it off. I have a boyfriend."

"I'm sure he likes your ass in those tights too."

"Hold up!!" Camas calls out in her loudest voice. "Pull over!"

Reeve and Cutter, riding in front, stop abruptly and turn around. They ride down to Camas.

"Are you OK?" Reeve asks, a bit out of breath.

Cutter looks at Reeve, "Uh oh."

Camas steps off of her bike and hands her bike to Reeve. "Hold this, please."

She walks back to Cashal. She finds two flat rocks and sets them side by side on the ground.

"What the hell are you doin', girly. The Italo team isn't far behind us. We need to get moving."

"Get off your bike and stand on these."

Cashal looks confused as he dismounts. "Don't get your panties in a bunch. I was just taking the piss out of ya."

"Now, Captain Kangaroo!"

"I'm Scottish, not Aussie!" he says, stepping up onto the stones. They are now eye to eye.

Camas turns to Reeve and Cutter, "You know, guys, we decided back in Sandglass we're a team. I'm in this to the finish. I'm giving it my all, but I want you to know that we're in the midst of a hashtag me too event right here." She turns to face Cashal. "Right now."

"Camas, I'm sorry, Cash...." Reeve says.

Camas interrupts him. "No apologies necessary. I just need to explain to all of you what 'me too' means to me."

"What is this?" Cashal says, stepping down off the rocks.

"Get your ass back up there! It won't take long!"

Cashal steps back up on the stones.

Camas stands up straight and speaks firmly. "To some, 'Me too' might mean going to the authorities of the adventure racing committee and letting them know that you're harassing me. 'Me too' to me means that the next time you mention any part of my physical body or sneeze at it, or fart at it, or tell an off-color joke within one hundred miles of me..." She stands four inches from him and stares him in the face. "...you smelly, slovenly gobshite, just when you're the weariest and can barely walk from exhaustion and lay your head down to sleep for those luxurious thirty-three minutes, I will have collected every pile of animal shit on and off the map, and it will somehow find its way into your cozy Scottish dungeon and dragons dreams. Let's just say you'll be crying for a new toothbrush in the morning. Got it, Red?!"

"Got it!" Cutter quickly responds.

"Not you, sweet Cutter," she turns back to Cashal. "Got it?!"

"Yes, lassie," Cashal says sheepishly.

"Yes, Camas," she corrects.

"Yes, Camas."

CHAPTER 27
LAGUNA DEL TIGRE NATIONAL PARK, GUATEMALA - 337,899 HA

(17.5730, -90.6773)

Tilly disembarks the freighter ship at Port of Freetown in Sierra Leone, her slight frame in stark contrast to the enormous vessel. She walks confidently off the boat, then winds through the maze of the customs line. Across the room, Rongo Jusu, a tall, muscular black man in his late twenties, holds a sign reading *Tilly DeMontagne*.

Tilly approaches him with a confused look. "I didn't call a driver. Did Camas hire you?"

"I'm not a driver," Rongo says with a New Zealand accent.

"Why are you holding a sign with my name?"

"What's that noise," Camas says with labored breathing as they approach the end of the cycling segment in St. Mary, Montana.

"Sounds like motorbikes," Cashal says, panting.

The motor sounds grow louder and louder. They round the bend and see the rest station and rows of motorbikes.

"Remember, that's why we have the panniers? We're riding between the parks," Reeve says.

"God forbid they give us anything restful," Camas says.

"Can you ride a motorbike?" Cashal asks pointedly.

"Of course," Camas says, walking to get a drink and snack from the race booth.

"Get your pretty ass... I mean, get over here. No time to rest!" Cashal yells.

"I'm just going to take a piss, Captain," Camas says as she runs, grabs a snack, and jumps into the porta-potty. Reeve and Cutter follow Camas as Cashal loads his bike and looks at the map.

"It's high tech! We can talk with each other," Camas says into her helmet mic as the Blueys ride down the highway. "We need music, though."

"We can talk, but we're likely being recorded because they're filming us," Reeve reminds her.

Camas looks around and up. She sees a helicopter with a camera and unzips her jacket to show some cleavage, smiles a big smile, and waves.

"Hey, I thought you were a woman of the times!" Cashal shouts over the engine noise. "There you go showing your titties."

"That's the point. They're my breasts, and I can do what I want with them. Not you or anyone else!"

"Did you get the parks from Hare, Cash?" Reeve asks.

"We're headed to Grand Teton next. It's an eight-hour ride if we're lucky."

"Shit," Camas says.

"Embrace the pain, sunshine," Cashal responds.

"From there, we'll go south to Dinosaur, then east over to

Rocky Mountain. We'll need to keep an eye on the weather, but from there, south to Sand Dunes, southwest to Chaco, then back north a bit to Mesa Verde and Hovenweep, finishing up in Canyonlands and ending at the Grand Canyon."

"I like that Chaco, Mesa, and Hovenweek are pretty close together," Cutter says.

"Sounds good," Reeve says.

The Blueys ride down the highway on the motorbikes.

"I see a lot of off-road around here. Why don't we stop and check the map?" Camas says into her helmet mic.

"I checked the map," Cashal grunts.

"You checked all 451 miles of the route when I took a piss?" Camas challenges.

"You girls are slow widdlers, so yes, I managed to map the 725 kilometers all by myself. Me, myself, and I, your captain."

Camas shakes her head. She turns off her mic and says to herself, "They didn't give us these dirt bikes for nothing."

"Liam called me to meet you," Rongo says.

"I told him I didn't need a bodyguard," Tilly says defiantly, looking up at him.

"I was born here. Maybe I can just hang out with you for a little bit."

Unsmiling, "If you must." Tilly picks up her pack and walks towards a line of taxis. A group of drivers rush up and circle her.

"I need a taxi," Tilly says, looking around at them.

The drivers are shouting with demonstrative arm movements. A couple of them grab her arm to try to lead her to their cabs. Tilly looks confused amidst the chaotic shouts. Rongo steps up, shakes the cabbies loose from Tilly, raises his hand, and calls out in Kiro. A cab pulls up. Rongo opens the door, and Tilly scoots over in the back seat as Rongo follows.

"Where to?" Rongo asks.

"I'm not sure. I'm going to see the Ministry of the Environment, but my appointment isn't until this afternoon."

"Take us to Tacugama Chimpanzee Sanctuary," Rongo calls.

Four motorbikes race off-road in the distance. Camas pulls out a small telescope between her breasts and sees them riding up and down a nearby hill.

"Hey, captain, oh, captain."

"What now, Cama-linda?"

"Don't look now but looks like the Blenheim Blizzards got the off-road memo."

Reeve looks over to Cutter. They raise their eyebrows.

"That off-roading is fuckin' exhausting," Cashal says.

"Might be faster," Camas says.

"We're staying on the highway."

CHAPTER 28
VATNAJÖKULL NATIONAL PARK, ICELAND – 1,414,100 HA

(64.7843, -17.2091)

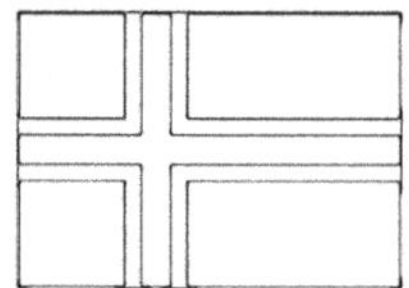

Television graphic and Hare's voiceover: *Parklands Enviro-Climate Challenge, Map of U.S. with a dot on all ten parks, Grand Teton's dot emphasized.*

"Grand Teton National Park is one of the most scenic national parks in the world, with the magnificent Teton Range rising nearly 7,000 vertical feet above the Jackson Hole Valley. The famous Snake River meanders along the valley floor. The park's iconic feature is Grand Teton peak at 13,770 feet."

The Brave Blueys and other Enviro Challenge teams raft the Snake River in challenging, churning whitewater. A drone camera captures a pair of men dropping a man in a kayak off the rock edge down into the Big Kahuna rapids. Hare looks down from the helicopter, and a herd of mule deer moves gracefully a few miles from the racers in the Snake River Canyon with Grand Teton peak in the distance.

"How's the race today?" Felice asks, standing outside a yurt overlooking the river on her phone.

"It's beautiful, and the teams are epic," Hare says flatly.

"Your voice doesn't match those words."

"Fremont called to tell me the ratings are shite."

"Uh, oh. What are you going to do about that?"

"I'm not sure. It's because the teams are all over the place for Score-O, and it's live, and we can't get the most harrowing shots like we usually do. I don't how to fix it."

"You'll figure it out."

"And I'm looking down on one of the most magnificent views of large wild animals. Elk or deer, I think, and in my hand is a report that says that the animals travel hundreds of miles and that between Yellowstone and Grand Teton there are nearly 18 million acres of their habitat."

"That sounds good."

"But over the last ten years, energy development has decreased the population by thirty percent, and the Department of Fish and Game say their populations are almost half of what they should be to be healthy."

"Tomorrow's my sacrificial raft ride with President Tweety. I'll ask him about it."

"What time?"

"He's golfing at Shooting Star in the morning, and then we're taking a slow float with his secret service guys from Deadman's Bar at 1:30."

"His team tried to get me to transport him in the helicopter, but I made an excuse. I owe you big time, my darling."

"Yes, you do. Chin up."

The Blueys run a moderate pace along a mountain trail lined with wildflowers near the tiny town of Moose, Montana, in

Grand Teton National Park. They see a log cabin chapel in the distance.

"There's the Chapel of the Transfiguration with the medallion. Camas, go retrieve it!" Cashal commands.

"We should get the medallion together," Camas responds.

"Why?" Cutter asks.

"I just feel that way."

Reeve walks with her to the chapel, then Cutter follows. The log cabin is rustic with old wooden pews and a large picture window behind the altar with a view of the cathedral peaks and Grand Teton. Cutter lowers down on his right knee and genuflects towards a cross at the altar. The light shines through the colorful stained glass windows. The ring-shaped four-inch race medallions are stacked on a vertical post in front of the tiny room.

Camas smiles at Reeve and Cutter. "This is so pretty! Where's Cash-hole?"

"It's a church, Camas," Cutter admonishes.

"I'll go get him," Reeve says, exiting the chapel.

"Are you spiritual, Camas?" Cutter asks.

"No. I don't think so, anyway. I always figure that Tilly has enough spirituality for both of us. How about you?"

"I'm a recovering Catholic, but I'm grateful to have been brought up with all that. It gave me a language of spirituality. I also like the rituals if they happen to fit at the moment. When I genuflect, I'm connecting to spirit, not being a Catholic."

"I've tried to talk to God, and I never heard anything back."

The door opens. Cashal looks frustrated.

"Cash, it's just one more minute," Reeve says.

Cashal puts his pack down and shuffles solemnly to join the group.

"OK, I'm here. Grab the god damn medallion," Cashal grunts.

"No, we all need to take it at the same time," Camas says.

"You're crazy."

Camas puts her hand on top of the medallion, then Reeve and Cutter follow. They look at Cashal.

"Come on, man," Cutter says.

Reluctantly, Cashal puts his hand on top of Cutter's.

"One, two, three Brave Blueys! OK?"

They nod.

Camas counts, "One, two, three..."

"Brave Blueys!" Cutter, Camas, and Reeve smile as they lift off the medallion.

Cashal turns and walks out, grumbling under his breath. Reeve shrugs. He and Cutter walk outside.

Camas puts the medallion in her pack. She turns around to look once more at the chapel. "This would be a sweet spot to tie the knot," she says to herself.

CHAPTER 29

POLLINO NATIONAL PARK, ITALY - 192,500 HA

(39.9413, 16.1223)

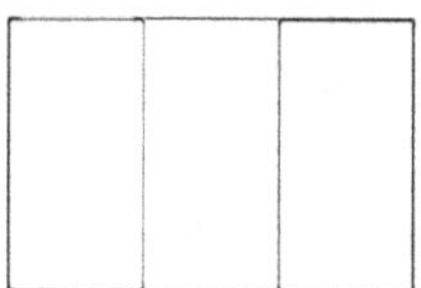

"That was amazing. Thank you for the tour. I hope they can save the chimps," Tilly says solemnly, looking out the cab window.

"You're welcome. Some musicians and artists have made videos to try to educate the population to stop clear-cutting and killing chimpanzees for food. Jane Goodall visited last year too."

"Is it working?"

"It's helped awareness. The key message is that if we don't protect the forest, there won't be chimps or fresh water."

"Or a planet. The forest is so beautiful here."

The cab travels from the Western Area Peninsula National Park towards Freetown.

"You looked so serious when you got off the ship. I thought this might cheer you up."

"It worked. How can you be serious watching chimps play?"

Rongo smiles.

"I'm sorry about earlier," Tilly offers.

"It's OK. I understand."

"How do you know Liam?"

"We played rugby together in New Zealand. I still play there for the national team, but I'm from Sierra Leone. My parents and I were refugees to New Zealand during the civil war. Why are you here?"

"I'm not sure exactly. A woman who seemed pretty wise asked me why I was just interested in the countries with good green ratings and not the ones with the poorest. It made me question that."

"When I was young, all of those hillsides you see were covered in forest."

Tilly looks out and sees barren hills with ramshackle housing.

"Why are those houses so dilapidated and the environment so degraded?"

"It's complicated, but in a nutshell, it's due to war, corruption, and poverty. What do you know about Sierra Leone?"

"I read that the civil war took place from 1991 to 2002."

"That's right. We could spend hours talking about that war, but the country is rich in diamonds, and it's caused problems. Sierra Leone should have been one of the world's richest countries. It's blessed with resources, including gold and diamonds, but it's one of the world's poorest."

Rongo pulls into a parking space. They walk into the lobby of a multi-story office building. The Minister of the Environment, a middle-aged Sierra Leonean woman in a skirt and blazer, greets them at the top of the steps. They shake hands and make introductions.

"Follow me, please," the minister says, walking out of the building.

Rongo and Tilly follow her down the city street. Local vendors offer them street food and trinkets. They turn a corner, and in the distance is a large hill bordering the city with a vast swath of dirt on the side, no vegetation or housing.

"That is the area of the 2017 mudslide that killed over one thousand people," the minister says.

"Oh, my God!" Tilly exclaims. "How in the world did that happen?"

"Unbridled development, shoddy construction, and corrupt officials."

"What's also sad is that many countries came to help the victims, but the government still sits on most of the money, " Rongo adds.

"They claim they don't want the people to have too much -- that it could cause them problems. It's a tragedy," the minister says.

"There's no way to get it to them?"

"We're trying," the minister says solemnly. "This way, please."

The minister walks into an ornate bank and speaks with a man at a desk. He leads the them towards the back of the building. The minister motions for Rongo and Tilly to follow. An armed security guard stands close by. The bank manager opens a safety deposit box, pulls out a metal box, and sets it on the counter. The minister lifts the lid. Clear sparkling gems, some set in rings, fill the box.

"Are those diamonds?" Tilly whispers with wide eyes.

"Yes, over 1,000 of them. The number of people who died in the mudslide. When word got out about the disaster and its connection to the corrupt diamond trade, people around the world donated their diamonds to help the victims."

"Wow."

"Trouble is they're not doing the people any good in here," the minister says.

Tilly gazes at the diamonds, and tears stream down her face.

The minister leads Rongo and Tilly walk back out onto the street. Tilly reaches over to take a bottle of water from a street vendor. Rongo grabs her arm.

"Don't drink that water," the minister says.

Camas leans down to fill her water bottle in a stream. Reeve reaches down and grabs her arm.

"Don't drink that water," Reeve says.

"It's crystal clear," Camas responds.

"Use your filter. If you get sick, you'll slow us all down." Cashal says.

CHAPTER 30

TASSILI N'AJJER NATIONAL PARK, ALGERIA – 7,200,000 HA

(25.8136, 8.1339)

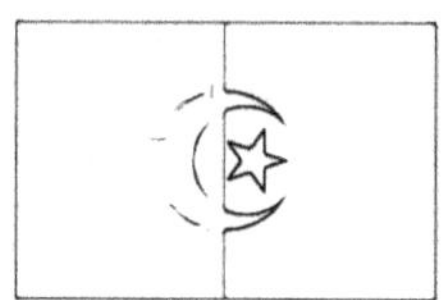

Television graphic and Hare's voiceover: Parklands Enviro-Climate Challenge, Map of U.S. with a dot on all ten parks, Dinosaur National Monument's dot emphasized.

"Dinosaur National Monument straddles Colorado and Utah and is renowned for the fossils of dinosaurs that remain embedded in the rocks and canyon walls. The park's iconic feature is the Gates of Lodore, where the Green River enters a dramatic, deep, red-walled canyon."

Hare extends out of the helicopter. "The athletes are racing over dinosaurs! Dinosaur National Monument contains over 800 paleontological sites in total and is home to petroglyphs and pictographs left behind by the Fremont people from over 1,000 years ago."

He leans back into his seat. The cameraman follows.

"Damn. No wonder the ratings are crap. We're supposed

to be showing the majesty of the terrain, and the air looks like downtown L.A."

"Are you feeling OK? I know it's a rough ride."

"I'm OK," Tilly says, looking out the window of the bus.

"We'll take this bus to Kenema where we'll spend the night. Then we'll take motorcycle taxis over the Liberian border, where we might need to partake in a bit of bribing for our convenience. Then we'll take a taxi from Bo Waterside to Monrovia."

Rongo waits for Tilly to respond. She continues looking out the window.

"I thought I'd get a response about the motorcycles or the bribing. Are you sure you're OK?"

"Yes, thanks. I just had a bad dream last night."

"I'm sorry. Do you want to talk about it?"

"I saw people in the mudslide."

"Oh, goodness."

"But they weren't in mud. They were in a blue ocean of diamonds. They weren't panicked. They were swimming towards me through the glittering diamonds. A thousand people swimming towards me, calling out." Tilly's eyes fill with tears. "The sounds were muffled and sounded like whales singing. I couldn't understand the words. I just felt their sadness."

Tilly sobs into her hands. Rongo puts his arm around her gently.

Sarah walks with Thomas under a thirty-foot pink dinosaur statue whose sign reads *Vernal - Utah's Dinosaur Land.*

She texts Tilly, *I'm trying to coordinate the locations for the protests, but I'm having trouble finding out where the race leaders are.*

Tilly stands with Rongo on the open veranda of a colorful two-story home converted to a guest house in a coastal neighborhood in Monrovia. She texts back, *OK, let me see what I can find out. Stand by.*

"Darn!" Tilly says.

"What's wrong?" Rongo asks.

"A friend is trying to protest at a big race for some media attention."

"What's the cause?"

"Clean water for people of color."

"That's ironic."

"How's that?"

"In Liberia, only twenty-five percent of the population has access to clean water, and only fifteen percent has access to sanitation services. Eighteen percent of all deaths are related to illnesses caused by poor water and sanitation."

Tilly looks at her water bottle. "Water seems so basic, but it's precious."

"How's she going to crash the race?"

"That's the trouble. The cameras are on the lead groups, but she doesn't know how to get just ahead of those,"

"I might be able to help."

"How? We're in Africa."

"Not to sound cocky, but the New Zealand teams are always in the lead in adventure racing. My brother-in-law's in the race, and my sister will know where he is from his GPS. They can't communicate, but she can see his dot on the map."

"That would be awesome."

"Samba will appreciate the cause."

"That's a pretty name."

"How do you know where the athletes will be next?" Thomas asks Sarah. Thomas's old olive green 1969 CJ5 Camper leads a convoy of eight vehicles, mostly old models, including two vans covered with colorful bumper stickers with political and environmental slogans.

"We don't, but we know the New Zealand team is in the lead and coming to Dinosaur National Monument next. They visited the most significant sights at Glacier and Grand Teton, so I'm guessing they'll pass through the Gates of Lodore. Sounds very Lord of the Rings," Sarah says.

"Reminds me of a poem."

"Look! There's the race support crew!"

Thomas slows down, pulls the jeep into a gravel parking area, and parks. The rest of the caravan parks one by one alongside.

Sarah texts Samba, *We're at the Lodore Campground and Ranger Station at Dinosaur. Where's your brother?*

Samba texts, *Looks like he's about 30 miles away.*

Thanks!

"There are some spectators over there. Can you text everyone to blend in until the media moment? I'll signal them when it's time."

"Got it," Thomas says, tapping his phone.

Stacks of deflated kayaks and paddles rest on the shore of the Green River. Thomas takes Sarah's hand, and they walk down the river away from the group as they wait for the racers to arrive. The water sparkles between the tall rock walls on either side of the river.

"'How does the water come down at Lodore?' My little boy asked me.'"

Sarah turns to him, surprised. They continue walking as Thomas recites.

"'Thus, once on a time; And moreover he tasked me to tell him in rhyme. Anon, at the word, there first came one daughter, and then came another, to second and third the request of their brother, and to hear how the water comes down at Lodore, with its rush and its roar, as many a time they had seen it before...'"

Sarah giggles. "What's that?!" She faces Thomas, excited to hear the answer.

"It's an old poem titled The Cataract of Lodore by the English poet Robert Southey who also wrote Goldilocks and the Three Bears."

"Wow."

"In 1869, John Wesley Powell, led a dangerous expedition from Wyoming to Nevada and named this The Gates of Lodore after the poem. They were the first recorded passage of white men through all of the Grand Canyon. They had many hardships including near-drownings and loss of boats, but they returned with the first detailed descriptions of this canyon country."

"First white man's description."

"True."

"Go on!" Sarah says, grabbing both of his hands and waiting.

Thomas smiles at her enthusiasm. He continues, "'So I told them in rhyme, for of rhymes I had store; and 'twas in my vocation for their recreation that so I should sing; because I was Laureate to them and the King. From its sources which well in the tarn on the fell; from its fountains in the mountains, its rills and its gills; through moss and through brake, it runs and it creeps for a while, till it sleeps in its own little lake.'"

The beautiful Green river travels through the canyon.

"'And thence at departing, wakening and starting, it runs through the reeds, and away it proceeds, through meadow and glade, in sun and in shade, and through the wood-shelter, among crags in its flurry, helter-skelter, hurry-skurry...'"

There is a loud cheer as the crowd at the campground hears the sound of motorocycles in the distance. Sarah and Thomas run back to the group. Four motorcycles arrive carrying the dusty-faced Benheim Blizzards.

Hare's assistant, race director, Stacey, a young athletic woman with short brunette hair in a ponytail, ball cap and sunglasses motions to the athletes. "Park there and leave the keys in the ignitions!" she shouts.

"Where in the world is Hare?! Where are the cameras?" Sarah asks Thomas.

Sarah runs up to Stacey. "Where's Hare Finnish?"

"He's at Hell's Half Mile, where the action will be. And who the hell are you?"

Sarah turns back to Thomas and her group. "Shit! No TV cameras here." Sarah shouts.

CHAPTER 31

SAPO NATIONAL PARK, LIBERIA – 180,365 HA

(5.4603, -8.4404)

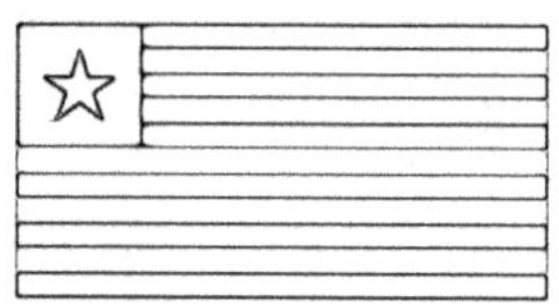

Rongo and Tilly travel through Sapo National Park in a battered ancient Renault sedan bush taxi driven by a young Liberian man wearing a Lonestar Liberia t-shirt.

"My, this rig is a mechanical miracle on wheels. I love that they've extended its life. Just not sure how much longer the pieces will hold together with the twine, wire, and duct tape," Tilly says.

"My ass... excuse me," Rongo corrects, "my bottom is touching metal."

"Here, take my neck pillow," Tilly offers.

"Thanks! What happened to your appointment?"

"Turns out the head of conservation at the Forest Development Authority couldn't meet me."

"Maybe he got word from Sierra Leone."

"I was polite and respectful."

"Yes, but sometimes people like to spin their own environmental stories."

"Same in the U.S."

"What do you know about Sapo?"

"I read that Liberia was in a 14-year civil war ending in 2003. Also, that the local Sapo people revere the chimpanzees, and it's taboo to hunt them."

The taxi turns a corner, and they hear an animal screeching. It gets louder and louder as they travel further down the road.

"Oh my goddess. What's that noise?"

"Just an animal in a trap. It's nothing," the driver says.

"It's not nothing. Stop the car!" Tilly shouts.

The driver continues down the bumpy road.

"Man, stop the car," Rongo says forcefully.

Rongo hands the driver money. "Don't leave. We'll be back. Tilly, hand me the jungle survival kit."

"We have a jungle survival kit?" Tilly looks around. "This?!"

"Yes!"

Tilly tries to open her door, but it is welded shut. "Damn jalopy!" She scoots out the opposite door, pulling the heavy duffel across the seat and out of the car.

Rongo takes it from her quickly, and they walk through the jungle towards the noise. Rongo sets the bag down, then bends over to open it. Inside the bag, Tilly can see a water filter straw and purification tablets, a butane lighter and waterproof matches in a ziplock bag, a fixed blade knife in a weathered sheaf, a fire striker, small kindling with some pre-charred cotton, a pocket knife, a knife sharpener, small nylon rope, compass, fish hooks and line, a small flashlight, alcohol wipes, diarrhea pills, antibiotic ointment, butterfly sutures, insect repellent, solar blanket, needle and thread, and a roll of Liberian dollars.

"Wow. That is a survival kit! I think my best friend could've used something like this in her race."

Rongo reaches down into the bag, pulls out binoculars,

and lifts them to his eyes. "Shit! There, can you see?" he says as he hands the binoculars to Tilly.

Tilly looks. "I can't see anything."

"Just to the left of that cotton tree. Lower, lower…"

"It's a deer or a goat," Tilly says.

"Looks like a duiker."

Rongo takes the larger knife out of the duffel. "Stay here."

"No, I'm going with you. I'd rather walk back to Monrovia than get back in that tin can without you."

"Fine," Rongo says as he walks into the bush towards the animal.

"You're bringing a knife?"

"I'd bring a pistol hiking into the jungle, but personal weapons are illegal in Liberia."

"I'm glad they're illegal. Very civilized. But why do we need a knife?"

"Tilly, you said you had to come with me."

Tilly is silent as they climb through thick grass and brush. They arrive at an animal that looks like a small antelope, with a tuft of hair between short spiked horns. It has labored breathing, and blood drips from the metal teeth of the trap holding its right hindquarter.

"Oh, no," Tilly says. "What in the world?"

"It's illegal to hunt for bushmeat, but the rangers don't carry guns, so it still takes place. A single hunter may set between two hundred and three hundred traps and not return for two to three weeks."

"Leaving the poor animal to this!"

"The meat is often sold to neighboring Sierra Leone and Cote d'Ivoire."

"We have to get it out of that."

"Tilly, he's likely too injured to survive."

"How do you know?" Tilly asks, eyes wide.

"Tilly, I think you should turn around and walk back towards the taxi."

Tilly and Rongo sit on handcrafted bamboo chairs on the patio in front of a thatch-roofed cottage overlooking a lagoon and forest near the Atlantic. The sun sets over the trees.

"I hope this place can fix up the little guy," Tilly says, looking out over the ocean.

"Me too."

"It's sad that this wildlife sanctuary is even needed for confiscated animals, but I'm grateful it's here."

Rongo nods.

"I was sure you were going to kill him."

"You'll learn that we don't like to kill things in New Zealand."

"I read that you're killing a bunch of rats and possums."

"That's true. There's a huge initiative to eradicate imported predators that have put about 2,000 species at risk."

"That's too bad for the rodents."

"Possums are marsupials."

"Noted. I can't believe you talked the taxi driver into letting us transport the duiker."

"I don't think he was worried we'd damage his taxi considering its condition."

Tilly laughs. "But still, it was a bloody injured animal."

"He wanted the fare to Libbassa Eco Lodge here in Marshall." Rongo puffs out his chest, "And was also intimidated by a Maori warrior."

"Huh? First you say you don't like to kill things, and now you're a warrior?" Tilly teases.

Rongo stands and walks to face Tilly in a bent knee

athletic stance. He makes a dramatic warrior face and extends his tongue in a wide-eyed expression as he does a traditional Maori haka with exaggerated, impressive gestures. Tilly raises eyebrows.

Camas, Reeve, Cashal, and Cutter follow the race director's instructions to park their motorbikes and rush to untie their pannier backpacks.

"Your supplies are there," Stacey points. Gather your required gear and make your way to the river to inflate your kayaks. Each team has one z-drag kit. If you don't know how to use it, see me before you launch!"

"I don't even know what it is. Let alone how to use it!" Camas shouts nervously.

"It's OK, Cam. It's a set of rope and carabiners that uses physics to split the weight of pulling a heavy boat into three. We'll show you," Reeve says in a comforting voice.

"Sounds like us pulling Cashal," Camas jokes.

"Very funny," Cashal says dryly. "Pay attention. We don't have time to waste."

"If the boat gets jammed between rocks with the pressure of the rushing water, for example, the z-drag can get it out," Reeve explains.

"Gosh, I hope that doesn't happen. What's the "z"?"

"That's the most important part. The z shape gets the three sections of the rope working together. The sliding prusik and pulleys keep the three rope sections equalized so they can all do their third of a job."

"I still don't get it."

"Of course you don't, blondie," Cashal says. "Come on. We're taking too much time. Let's get the hell out of here."

"It's just a few more minutes, Cash," Reeve says. "Let's be safe."

"Christ almighty. Hurry it up."

Reeve continues. "Let's pretend there is a big bucket of cement, and you pick it up. Then, I come over and hold it with you. It would be lighter, right?"

"Sure."

"Then Cutter comes and holds it with us."

"It would be lighter still."

"Yep. That's the z-drag. It cuts the amount of strength needed to pull a boat or person in the water by three. Here's let's make one."

"Reeve, come on, man," Cashal complains.

"Just a few more minutes."

Reeve and Cutter bend down, pull the contents of the z-drag kit out of its bag and begin the lesson.

"First, you'll build an anchor by wrapping the sling around a rock or tree."

Camas throws the rope around Cashal's leg.

"Hey!"

"Tie the ends of the sling together with a double fisherman's knot, like this."

"I don't know that knot."

"We are absolutely not teaching knots now," Cashal scowls.

"Alright. Camas, I'm sure we'll be crossing other rivers. I'll show you the knots tonight in camp."

"Then clip a carabiner and pulley through the sling, like this. This is the anchor carabiner."

Cashal stands firm with the rope around his leg. "Hurry the hell up!"

"Secure one end of this haul rope to the load. If we're freeing a boat, we'll want to tie it onto the far end of the boat. Now we run the working end of the rope through the anchor carabiner."

"OK," Camas says, watching intently.

"Now we need to make a prusik loop."

"I don't know how to make that either."

"Damn, lassie. Didn't you ever go climbin'?"

"Shut up, anchor ass."

"It's OK. I'll teach you that one later too." Reeve quickly makes the prusik loop and wraps it very close to the load. He clips another carabiner and pulley through a second prusik.

Cutter continues. "Now, run this working end of the rope through this second carabiner. This is the traveling prusik."

"We should be traveling!" Cashal shouts.

"Run the tail end of the rope through the prusik pulley and back towards Cashal, the anchor."

Camas pulls the rope.

"That's right," Cutter says. "Now, pull on the tail end of the rope in the same direction as the main line is pulling on the boat."

"I see the z!"

"You've got a z-drag!" Reeve says, smiling.

Camas is proud of herself. "Don't worry, guys. I promise I'll learn the knots. Thanks for the lesson! Cashal, thanks for being the 'drag' in the z-drag."

Cashal shakes the rope off his leg and grunts. "Repack that god damn kit, and let's roll."

"We're going to have to shut this boondoggle down if the ratings don't improve, Hare. Best case is you get to finish it to no viewers and no future races," Fremont says, pacing in front of an elementary school-age girls' volleyball game in

Manhattan Beach. He wears linen Bermuda shorts and loafers with no socks.

"Don't threaten me, you son of a bitch. The love of my life just breathed the same air as Don't Cry For Me Trumpentina to get these race locations, and we're not done yet!"

"Buddy, buddy... calm down."

"Don't condescend. Yes, we're long-term friends. I shouldn't have to remind you of that."

"I don't need reminding."

"Seems you do as you should be helping me get the resources to film the teams on the ground. We should have had that at the get-go."

"Well, we don't have it. I can't just go back and ask for forty more camera teams. Not just forty more cameras. Forty elite athlete camera teams that can keep up."

"That's bullshit. They don't all need to be elite. Just be able to drive a four-wheel drive, hike a distance, and be creative."

"And not sleep! It's too late. I've tried for even ten more camera teams, and the network just thinks it's throwing good money after bad."

Hare is quiet.

"Hare?"

"Give me a minute."

Fremont paces nervously with his phone to his ear.

"OK, get me 200 waterproof unlocked satellite phones with solar battery back-ups. Lightest you can find."

"What?!"

"Do you need me to repeat it?"

"How are we going to pay for that?"

"You're going to pay for that out of your producer cut when we boost the ratings or your daddy's trust fund. I don't give a fuck which. And we need ten choppers for tomorrow morning to drop the phones to the racers."

"Now you've gone absolutely nuts!" The well-coifed volleyball parents scowl at Fremont.

"We're between two hundred and three hundred miles of an air force base and an air force academy. Call in some favors and get the helos."

Sarah is upset. She hurries back towards their Jeep. Thomas tries to put his arm around her to comfort her, but she walks too fast and shrugs his hand away.

"There's no TV camera, but I can film you," Thomas offers.

"It's not the same. Just a bunch of tie-dye in the middle of nowhere."

"Not just tie-dye. Parklands Enviro-Climate goddesses and warriors."

Sara smiles. Her phone buzzes. She looks down at a text from her mother, *I'm in Phoenix with the activists ready to march. We've got protesters in L.A., Houston, San Diego, Sacramento, Chicago, Philly, and Denver. Waiting for your signal to march and film.*

Sarah is quiet, thinking. "Okay!" She raises her hand, and the caravan group pulls out military-style gas masks and signs on posts reading *Spoiled Parklands* with the O, I, and L in bright red letters, *Why can't I breathe in the wilderness?* and *Stop unravelling air and water protections for fossil fuels!*

Sarah texts Durga, *We're on. Go!*

Sarah speaks powerfully inside her M40 gas mask with protesters holding picket signs behind her as Thomas films.

"We're here at the Gates of Lodore at Dinosaur National Monument where the air should be pristine, but year after year, the Uinta Basin reports serious air quality issues. Just last year, Uintah County, Utah, received a failing grade from the American Lung Association. And what's causing the dirty air, you may be wondering? Neighboring oil and gas operations are the largest source of air and climate pollution..."

The Blueys finish blowing up their kayaks, load their boats, and put on life vests.

Camas looks over to the protesters, "What the hell?"

"Let's roll!" Cashal shouts.

"Camas, are you OK?" Reeve asks.

"I think I know those beatnik hippies," Camas says, looking at Sarah and Thomas. She raises her arm to get Sarah's attention, but Sarah doesn't see her.

The Blueys launch their boats and paddle out into the rushing river. Motorcycle engines are heard in the distance.

Thomas moves his phone closer to Sarah for better sound.

"Since taking office, Forty-Five's administration offered about 19 million acres of public land for oil and gas leasing. That's bigger than the entire state of West Virginia! And proposed slashing protections on 24 million acres. A study shows that if things run their course, by 2050, the new drilling would add 120 billion metric tons of carbon pollution, or the equivalent of the lifetime carbon dioxide emissions of 1,000 coal-fired power plants! Just when we need to phase out emissions, the U.S. is moving faster than any other country to expand oil and gas. It's our goddess-given right to breathe clean air and drink clean water."

The group behind Sarah begins chanting, "Clean air and water is our fight, green amendment bill of rights! Clean air and water is our fight, green amendment bill of rights!"

Thomas lowers the camera. He walks over, carefully pulls up Sarah's gas mask, and kisses her.

Stacey notices the protesters as she guides two more teams from their motorbikes to the kayaking launch. "What in the world?!"

She texts Hare with a photo of the group. *Hare, we have some people in gas masks with pickets at Gates of Lodore.*

Hare texts back, *Roger*.

Hare shakes his head and smiles. He says to himself, "Well, the goddamn ferals arrived right on time."

CHAPTER 32
AÏR AND TÉNÉRÉ NATIONAL NATURE RESERVE, NIGER – 7,736,000 HA

(19.5738, 9.2046)

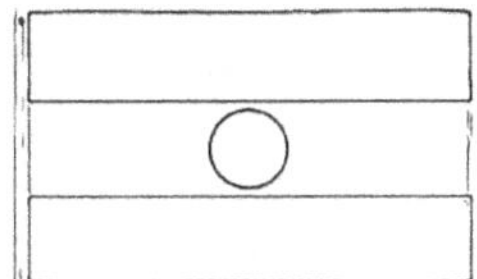

Chants of "Clean air and water is our fight, green amendment bill of rights!" fill the air across the United States. Civil rights, environmental, and climate organizations march for a green amendment to the U.S. Constitution on the sacred grounds of Native American peoples.

Greater Los Angeles, California, #1 worst ozone air quality, #4 worst particulate air quality, 69% people of color. Hundreds of green amendment supporters march down Hollywood Boulevard. Jane Fonda links forearms with Rita Morena holding a sign reading *Green Amendment #FireDrillFridays* moving along a river of rainbow afros, UCLA and USC sweatshirts, Phlemens cargo pants, business suits, and yoga capris. A large earth-painted beach ball dangles on a pole above the marching crowd. School-age kids carry an *Amigos de Los Rios Emerald Necklace* banner. Diverse people wear sunglasses of all shapes and sizes, and their tees proudly carry hopeful words of healthy earth, clean air, and sparkling water... *Breath Southern California, Climate Cents, Ballona Wetlands, Los Angeles Waterkeepers, River LA, Topanga Creek Watershed, Tree People, Burbank Green Alliance.* Birders with binoculars, professors, community leaders, politicians, children holding parents' hands, and transients pushing their homes chant, "Hey ho, hey ho, climate change has got to go! Hey ho, hey ho, climate change has got to go!"

Native American tribes: Chumash, Alliklik, Kitanemuk, Serrano, Gabrielino Luiseno Cahuilla, and the Kumeyaay.

Greater Houston, Texas, #14 worst ozone air quality, #22 worst particulate air quality, 64% people of color. Waves break onto a long, white, sandy beach in front of a 1950's-modern round structure with tall windows and undulating roofline. The Sylvan Beach Pavilion, beat down by eight hurricanes, watches the horizon. Waters creep up slowly inch by inch, almost two feet since the building was constructed in 1956 due to global warming and land sinking from groundwater and fossil fuel extraction. Twenty-seven miles away, a college-age girl with long straight brunette hair in two neatly braided ponytails and a Stetson cowboy hat stands with a crowd of protesters around Hermann Plaza reflection pond at Houston City Hall. She wears a bright yellow T-shirt with *Sunrise Movement* on the front, tucked into her Lee jeans, and carries a vibrant yellow sign *What IS your plan?* Pete Buttigieg, amidst volunteers from Artist Boat, Galveston Bay Foundation, Houston Peace and Justice Center, and other organizations, wears a *Bike Houston* shirt and carries a sign reading *Irreversible green protections! Green Amendment Bill of Rights.* An elderly man with a weathered face under a grimy, sweaty cowboy hat, wearing a western shirt and cowboy boots, carries a tall vertical sign that reads, *Stop climate denial. Save Galveston. If I wanted to paddle home, I'd live in Venice! Green Amendment now!*

Native American tribe: Akokisa

Greater San Diego, California, #6 worst particulate air quality, 55% people of color. A blonde young man steps out of Bird's Surf Shed, a half-circle Quonset hut with a row of colorful boards in front. He carries a vintage Hansen Sole Rider surfboard under his arm and jumps on a skateboard to join a large group of protesters in front of the Spanish revival-style San Diego Administration building. He sees a group of his friends carrying signs reading *The seas are rising, and so are we! Surfrider Foundation.* A row of colorful, classic low-rider cars and trucks line the street with signs: *Live slow, ride low,* and *No hay plan(eta) B. Green Amendment.* Protesters of all ages, colors, and backgrounds chant, "Se ve, se siente, la Tierra está caliente!"

Native American tribes: Kumeyaay / Diegueño, Payoomkawichum (Quechnajuichom / Luiseño and Acjachemen/Juaneño), Kuupiaxchem/Cupeño, and the Cahuilla.

Greater Sacramento, California, #5 worst ozone air quality, #18 worst particulate air quality, 47% people of color. In an increasingly hot city plagued by too much commuter traffic, hundreds of bicycles ride along the Sacramento River Parkway bike trail with banners pinned to the back of their shirts and handlebars. *Green Bill of Rights is our Fight. Cycling action is climate action. This is a climate crisis. Burn fat, not oil!* They turn left off the bike trail onto a downtown city street. Cars honk in support or road rage as the hoard of cyclists slow traffic on their way to the State Capitol building. Governor Nevin Handsome greets the cyclists on the steps of the Capitol Building, where red-robed Extinction Rebellion activists with white paint on their faces line the edges of the green lawn. Like Greek gods dressed in the blood-red of their species, they link arms with solemn faces.

"I support a Green Amendment to the United States Constitution," Handsome says to the cyclist protesters.

News reporters film the Governor and the chanting crowd. "That's bullshit! Get off it! This planet's not for profit!"

Native American tribes: Nisenan, Maidu, Miwok (Me-Wuk), Patwin Wintun.

Greater Chicago, Illinois, #16 worst ozone air quality, #20 worst particulate air quality, 46% people of color population. A pretty black woman in her mid-thirties pulls a sign from the top of her dresser. *I can't breathe. Black Lives Matter.* She puts it on her dining room table with the words face down, pulls out a box of acrylic paints and a brush. She paints *I can't breathe. Green Amendment now!* Later she marches with over thirty environmental organizations and Chicago citizens from the Wrigley Building to City Hall. The group chants, "What do we want? Green Amendment! When do we want it? Now!"

Native American tribes: Potawatomi, Odawa, Sauk, Ojibwe, Illinois, Kickapoo (Kiikaapoi), Miami (Myaamia), Mascouten, Wea, Delaware, Winnebago, Menominee, and Mesquakie.

Greater Phoenix, Arizona, #7 worst ozone air quality, #7 worst particulate air quality, 45% people of color. Durga speaks to a group of protesters in front of the Art Deco Mission Revival-style Maricopa County Courthouse.

"We are now closer than ever to bringing our U.S. Constitution into the 21st century to confirm that clean air, water, and a healthful environment are just as important as one's equality or freedom of speech. Let's march to the Capitol!"

Durga pulls on an M40 military-style gas mask and raises a sign that reads, *Enough! Green Amendment now!* Youth climate activists, teachers, scientists, politicians, and concerned citizens move slowly down West Jefferson street holding signs reading *No Planet B, Green Amendment, Respect your mother, Be part of the solution, not the pollution.*

Native American tribes: Ak-Chin, Yavapai, Pima (Akimel Auauthm) and Maricopa (Xalychidom Pipaash)

Denver, Colorado, #10 worst ozone air quality, 35% people of color population. Protesters chant "Rebirth, realize, rethink, reawaken; give back to the earth what we have taken!" as they march from Union Station up the 16th Street Mall to the Colorado State Capitol. Flannel, beanies, yoga tights, environmental logo tees, pussy hats, overall cutoffs, trendy high-tops, cowboy boots, Allbird dasher running shoes all move along in procession. At the Capitol, compassionate bodies bounce, bob, and dance to the hip-hop rap of Xiuhtezcatl Martinez and DJ Cavem. Signs reading *Don't frack with our water, Mother Nature called. She called you a bitch,* and *Fight climate change or die frying* wave above the crowd.

Native American tribes: Southern Ute, Mountain Ute, Arapaho.

Greater Philadelphia, Pennsylvania, #23 worst ozone air quality, #12 worst particulate air quality, 38% people of color.

"I'm here at Belmont Plateau in Fairmont Park," a TV reporter says to the camera. "Olivier Clan will be speaking to a crowd of peaceful climate protesters. They're calling for a constitutional convention to pass the Green Amendment, Claire,"

Clair shares a split TV screen. "Experts say that could never happen. Did you ask him about that, Jerry?"

"Not yet." Jerry turns around as Olivier steps up to the mic. "Looks like he's starting!"

Protesters surround the stage carrying signs and wearing environmental t-shirts. *Fithydelphia Freedom, Brother. Philly Thrive Right to Breathe Campaign. Philly Sunrise Movement. Campaign for a Voice in PES Refinery Clean-up Now!. Birds sing in clean air Audubon Pennsylvania. Earth Quaker Action Team. Parked? Turn off your engine! Idle Free Philly. Divest from Destruction, Reinvest in Justice (Swarthmore Mountain Justice). Coal Kills Climate. Schuykill Canal Restoration.*

"Hello friends," Olivier calls out to the crowd. "We're here to call for an amendment to the United States constitution!"

The crowd cheers.

"Forty years ago, after reading Rachel Carson's Silent Spring, Wisconsin Senator Gaylor Nelson called for immediate action to protect the earth, inspiring the first Earth Day. In 1970, right where we stand today, Philadelphia hosted the most impressive celebration for mother earth. Over 25,000 people gathered. Allen Ginsberg's poetry and Native American band Redbone's haunting chants filled the air. Senator Muskie spoke and soon after introduced the Clean Air Act and worked to pass the Clean Water Act."

The crowd cheers.

"And while we've made progress, we can no longer wait to

confirm clean air and water as an inalienable right. While my friend Murabai Rodriguez tells me his asthmatic baby now sleeps through the night, and his wife's chronic headaches are less frequent now that the nearby sprawling Philadelphia Energy Solutions PES refinery site is defunct, clean-up will take over ten years. Abatement of asbestos wrapped around pipeline that could connect Philly to Florida and removal of 3,000 tanks and vessels and more than 100 buildings is the gargantuan task. This old PES refinery is just one of about 135 oil refineries nationwide. We want a say in the remediation process, the redevelopment, and the allocation of jobs. There've been too many secrets in the toxic soup, and we can't allow cutting of corners in reparations of the air, water, and soil of our cities and communities!"

The crowd cheers.

"And while we may have waited forty years for the cast of the Broadway musical Hair to reunite here with us,..."

Tie-dyed, bohemian-inspired performers run to join Olivier onstage wearing leather fringed jackets and vests, daisy chains, rose-colored glasses, with large round afros and long hair.

"...we can't wait another forty years for clean air, water or racial environmental equity!"

The crowd cheers more loudly.

Music starts, and the performers move towards the front of the stage.

"Here's the cast of Hair performing Air!"

Music plays and the performers sing.

"Welcome! sulphur dioxide. Hello! carbon monoxide. The air, the air ... is everywhere. Breathe deep, while you sleep... breathe deep. Sing along!"

The crowd sings.

"Bless you, alcohol bloodstream. Save me, nicotine lung steam. Incense, incense... is in the air. Breathe deep, while you sleep... breathe

deep. Cataclysmic ectoplasm. Fallout atomic orgasm. Vapor and fume at the stone of my tomb. Breathing like a sullen perfume. Eating at the stone of my tomb. I'm looking rather attractive, now that I'm radioactive. Just watch me spark. I glow in the dark. Breathe deep, while you sleep... breathe deep, deep, deep, de-deep!"

The performers and audience cough dramatically.

Native American tribes: Lenape, Susquehannock, Shawnee, and Iroquois.

Air Force helicopters fly over the Parklands Enviro-Climate Challenge teams and lower a net carrying a breadbox-sized box down to each captain.

Stacey calls Hare. "The sat phones are dropped."

CHAPTER 33
LIMPOPO NATIONAL PARK, MOZAMBIQUE – 1,123,300 HA

(-23.6548, 32.1746)

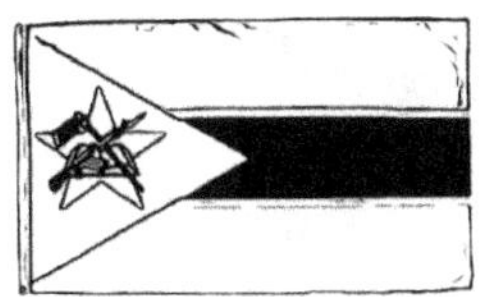

*P*arklands Enviro-Climate Challenge TV graphic and Hare *voiceover: Map of U.S. with a dot on all ten parks, Rocky Mountain National Park's dot emphasized.*

"Rocky Mountain National Park is one of the highest national parks in the U.S., 415 square miles atop the Continental Divide. Its sixty mountain peaks, over 12,000 feet and up to 14,259 feet high, result in world-renowned scenery. The park's iconic feature is Crestone Needle, a fourteener in the Sangre de Cristo Range of the Rockies."

The Blueys rollerski with intensity uphill along the paved Trail Ridge Road in Rocky Mountain National Park. Another team is about one mile ahead from a birds-eye view, and several other racers follow a few miles behind. The sun shines bright with small patches of snow on the edge of the road. Reeve skis the pavement in the lead, followed by Camas, then Cashal. Cutter brings up the rear wearing a headband to dam their river of sweat. Reeve wears a dirt-smudged ball cap with a bicycle wheel and syringa flower in the center. Cashal hums a loud Gaelic tune and wears a lightweight wool Tam beret with a small pom-pom.

Reeve arrives at the crest of a ridge and raises his hands. "Whoop!" he shouts in triumphant relief.

Cashal rollerskis in sweeping skate moves to gain on Camas. He races up alongside her, then passes.

"Are you grunting or singing, señor Stonehenge?" Camas says, exerting to keep up.

"Stonehenge is in England. The Scottish stones are the much older Calanais Standing Stones!"

"Well, if you're going to sing, you could at least add a bit of melody if your old stones are going to be standing!" Camas says as she finds a new gear.

Cashal and Camas race to the crest of the hill, arriving together. They turn around at the top as Cutter climbs the final yards.

"Come on, Cutter! Let's fly before Hare's call," Cashal shouts as he heads downhill.

The team laughs and shouts, "Blueys!" as they rollerski joyfully down, making tight turns and taking ski-race low tucks on the straightaways.

Hare and his camera crew stand at the bottom of Crestone Needle rock face in Rocky Mountain National Park.

Hare calls Stacey. "Defcon 1. Radio the captains of all teams to be in one place with their sat phones and the box they received at 800 hours. Over."

"Roger."

Hare motions to the camera team. "Roll!"

The two cameramen begin filming.

"Behind me is the iconic Crestone Needle, first climbed

in 1916 by Colorado professors Albert Ellingwood and Eleanor Davis. These two are thought to be among the first to practice belayed climbing in the United States. The Parklands Enviro-Climate Challenge racers will follow in these climbing pioneers' footsteps as they pair up to attempt to climb the dangerous Ellingwood Arete route."

Hare points to the rock face. "Most fatalities on the Needle occur here. A 'crux' of a climb is the part of the climb with the greatest danger. On this classic, the crux is the headwall section, requiring four pitches over a distance of about 150 feet. Lucky for the athletes, they'll have a nice crack to help them. We don't expect any accidents, but the teams are feeling the strain and exhaustion of the race, so we'll have rescue teams ready for any racers who get stranded on the Ellingwood Ledges."

Hare pauses. "Cut! Get some shots of the cliff!"

Hare walks away to call the racers. The Blueys stand at the side of the road in their roller skis, huddled around Cashal's phone.

"Teams, good work! Many of you are at the fourth park, with others not far behind. This call is to tell you that your gear at the climb in Rocky Mountain Park will include tri-cams, cams from 0.5 to 4, mid to large stoppers, 24-inch runners. You'll also be required to use twin ropes at the crux. For those of you who don't know how to use hexes, the race support will train you at the foot of the climb. You'll carry the hexes in case you encounter wet or icy cracks. Take it slow. Be precise."

Hare pauses. "One recent climber free fell 25 feet because two of his pieces came out, and only one held, along with his partner's belay. Got it? Text Stacey the words 'Creston gear, roger' so we have your affirmative response on this gear communication."

"God damn. That sounds fuckin' scary. And 'hex' just

sounds like a bad word overall to use when your climbing," Camas says from the side of the highway.

"Shush," Cashal says firmly.

"Just sayin'."

Hare continues. "Unpack the box you received if you haven't already."

Fifty teams on trails, roller skis, motorbikes, bicycles, lying under tarps resting, eating, parked on riverbanks, and injured at the race support station unpack their new box from the helicopter. They pull out four phones and four solar battery packs.

"We are changing the rules."

The athletes listen intently.

"From now on, you'll all have full access to a satellite phone. Many of you have already gotten reconnaissance from locals or other teams. Now you can use all available mapping and app resources for food, fuel, route knowledge. In exchange for this upgrade in resources, we have a new requirement. Each person is required to take a photo or video of the best and worst events of the day. The worst can be the hardest, the most embarrassing, the most traumatic. Tears are good. The best is impressive and dramatic! Blood and sweat are good."

"Sounds like that seventies show —the thrill of victory, the agony of defeat," Camas says.

Cashal turns to Camas. "Shu...."

"Stop shushing me, Shetland pony!"

"And upload it within 24 hours to Stacey and tag @parklandschallenge. You've got solar chargers. Keep your phones charged! Any questions? That's rhetorical. Over and out!"

The Blueys continue rollerskiing down the hill.

Camas slows to tap the dial screen of her new phone.

"This is Reina."

"Hi, Reina. My name is Camas. We have a mutual friend, Tilly DeMontagne."

Camas stops.

"Oh, Tilly. Yes, she and her brother Moore helped defeat a nasty mine project in Alaska, Copper Cobra. "

"Yep."

"'Camas' did you say? Oh my goodness! Aren't you Raise it Red? Sexy Salmon with Camas?!"

"That's me."

"Nice work. What can I do for you?"

"I need your help."

"What is it?"

"Yesterday, I saw my friend Sarah Montana with a group of protesters chasing the Parklands Enviro-Climate race. They carried green amendment signs," Camas says.

"That's strange. I haven't caught any of that yet. I'm usually dialed in."

"That's the problem. She's out there in the boondocks, and other than a couple of videos, it hasn't broken out. I just got permission to use a phone, but I don't know if I'll see her again."

"The park rangers all have their live stream shows to promote the parks. I have some contacts. I'll see what I can do."

"Thanks, Reina!"

"I need a favor too."

"Name it."

"I've caught wind that they may be reopening the uranium mine at the Grand Canyon."

"No fuckin' way."

"Way."

"No way."

"Way."

Silence on the line.

"Can you keep your eye out when you get to the Canyon? It's a vast area, so I doubt you'll see anything but you never know."

"My eyes are blurry from dust, sweat, and bullshit, but sure."

Reeve stands at the top of Ellenwood Ledges as Camas climbs carefully up over the last rock ledge. She hugs him, then slumps down onto the ground, lying on her back.

"I'll join you in a minute. Just watching out for the guys," Reeve says.

"You're a good man, Reeve," Camas says, breathing heavily.

"You rock too, Camas. Nice climbing."

Camas staggers to a stand. "What a glorious view. Even though I think I might croak on this adventure, I've died and gone to heaven with this beauty."

Cutter and Cashal are heard approaching the top.

"I'll help them. Why don't you find the medallion? Cashal said it's 103 feet and 10 degrees southwest of the top of this crevice."

"OK."

Camas stumbles from exhaustion as she walks away from the cliff edge. Cutter climbs up over the ledge, followed by Cashal. They fall to their knees and crawl to lie down.

"I found it! It's over here!" Camas says.

"I can't believe we have to go down that mother too," Cutter says.

"Come over here!"

Cashal grumbles as he stands up and follows Reeve and Cutter.

Camas stands next to a rod in the center of a stone with medallions stacked on top near the ledges overlooking the Sangre de Cristo peaks.

"You know what to do," she smiles as she puts her hand on top of the medallion.

The guys put their hands, one on top of the other. They call out, "One, two, three...Bluey's!"

Camas sees that Cashal has a small smile. Then he turns serious. They hear other voices shouting from the face of the rock.

"Let's get back down that mountain!" Cashal shouts, walking back.

"Hey man, I don't think we have enough daylight," Reeve says.

"We'll freeze our asses off up here. Plus, the Kiwis are on our asses. I doubt the Blizzards will sleep."

"If we can make it down the crux in light, we should be OK," Camas offers.

"Are you sure, Camas?" Cutter asks.

"I'm the captain," Cashal asserts.

"Cash, it's intense. Life or death, man."

Cashal repeats the question slowly. "Are you sure, Camas?"

"I can do it."

"Then let's get the hell out of here!"

Sarah, Thomas, and protesters holding green amendment signs stand in front of the historic 1920s-era Holzwarth dude ranch lodge as Thomas films. A nearby park ranger shoots a live video of Sarah speaking.

"Visitors to Rocky Mountain National Park spend about

$306 million in the neighboring communities that serve the park and support over 4,300 jobs, but the pollution from oil and gas drilling is harming the park's ecosystems. New invasive grasses and pine bark beetles that kill millions of trees are some of the climate change effects. Increased wildfires threaten..."

Sarah pauses as helicopter blades chop loudly overhead. Thomas points his camera upward to the sky to see Hare leaning out the side as the aircraft lands nearby.

Sarah raises her voice over the noise. "Increased wildfires threaten visitors, animals, and nearby communities!"

Thomas stops filming. The park ranger walks away from the group towards the visitor building.

Hare jumps out of the helicopter and walks briskly towards them. His face is serious.

"Uh oh," Sarah says.

"Should we leave?" one of the protesters asks.

"It's OK," Thomas says. "We're not doing anything wrong."

"Good afternoon. Sarah Montana and Thomas Foolerin. Am I right?" Hare extends his hand.

"That's right," Thomas says, shaking his hand.

"Hare Finnish."

Sarah holds her hand out. "We're just leaving now," Sarah says nervously.

Hare shakes her hand, then reaches into his pocket. He pulls out a satellite phone and a solar battery pack and hands them to Thomas.

Thomas taps the phone, and a screen opens displaying a map of the Enviro-Climate Challenge race route as he and Sarah had seen on the race website. He looks closely and sees other dots. He taps one of them, and a pop-up note, *Camera 6,* appears.

"What is it?!" Sarah asks.

"The element of surprise, we could not achieve. The vastness of nature, brought us to our knees. We shoot ToeSock and Facebook Live shows to audience nil, but now we have access to TV cams' action just up the hill."

"What?!" Sarah asks, confused.

Hare turns and walks away. He steps up into the helicopter, looks back at Sarah and Thomas, and shouts with a fist in the air, "Clean air and water is our right. Green amendment is our fight!"

CHAPTER 34
ALONNISOS MARINE PARK, GREECE – 226,000 HA

(39.2711, 24.0488)

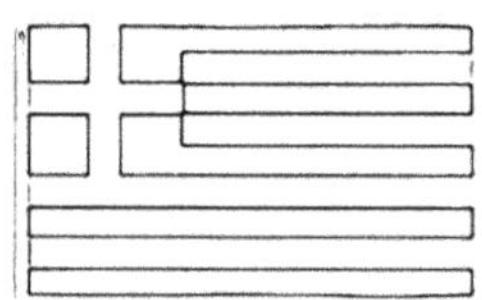

*P**arklands Enviro-Climate Challenge TV Graphic and Hare voiceover: Map of U.S. with a dot on all ten parks, Great Sand Dune's dot emphasized.*

"Great Sand Dunes National Park and Preserve is an International Dark Sky Park and contains the tallest dunes in North America. The rugged Sangre de Cristo mountain range provides a dramatic backdrop to the dunes, soaring to over 14,000 feet. The park's iconic feature is Star Dune, the tallest dune in North America, 750 feet from base to summit.

The sun sets over the magnificent sand mounds as the Blueys hike up a gigantic dune. A sandsurf board rests on each of their shoulders.

"The sun has set, and it's getting cold, but the sand is still scorching," Camas says.

"I think it's cooling down," Reeve replies.

The four trudge up the slippery dunes.

"Is this environmental?" Camas asks.

"We'll just roll you down the hill, princess," Cashal says.

"Very funny. Just asking.'"

"Sounds like whining to me."

"I think the wind and rain will reconstruct our trails," Reeve says.

Cutter pants heavily. "Just avoid the native grasses if you don't want to hurt them, Camas."

"Or fall flat on your face," Cashal adds.

Sand sparkles from the moonlight and thousands of stars in the dark sky as the team reaches the crest.

"Wow. Looks like champagne powder at Schweitzer! Let's jib until we see the trail," Cutter says.

Camas gives Cutter the thumbs up.

"It's a four-foot drop to the sand. Keep your weight low, " Cashal says, putting on his headlamp. "Oh wait, your womanly weight is already low."

"You come from a rock island. I come from the snow. We'll see who can board." She takes off her shoes and steps into the straps.

"I don't think we need the lamps, Cash," Reeve says.

"Reeve's right. It's bright enough with the stars," Cutter adds.

Cashal follows Camas's lead and removes his shoes. He takes off the headlamp.

"If I had asked, you'd have turned it brighter," Camas says. "Whooo-eeeh, your feet smell, man. Didn't you bring extra socks?"

"No."

Camas's nose scrunches from the smell. She hops sideways away from Cashal. "Hey, we have these phones. Let's sync our tunes!"

"That's frivolous. We'll waste our power. Not to mention,

this is a race, and here we are talking about music when we should be down the hill!"

"Music is as basic to the human body as food, captain cranky. Look, it already has ChoralAmp," Camas says, tapping her phone a couple of times. A melodic indie-rock song plays with an uptempo beat.

Reeve and Cutter pull out their race phones and tap to connect.

"It might help us warn off any animals, like the Kangaroo Rats," Reeve says.

"Ugh, alright." Cashal taps his phone to start the music.

"Hey, Cowabunga Camas! I'll film you for Hare," Cutter holds up his phone.

Camas makes love to the camera, then jumps off the ridge down onto the dunes. "Dropping!" she shouts.

She lands with skill and sandsurfs confidently. Reeve follows her, then Cashal and Cutter.

The Blueys surf down over the warm dunes. There is a low humming in the background.

"Listen," Camas calls, slowing. She stops. "Can you hear that?"

The men stop. They hear a beautiful buzz-like humming.

"I've read about this," Reeve says. "It's a natural phenomenon as air is pushed through millions of tumbling sand grains during an avalanche, or in this case surfing."

Camas starts humming along with the noise. Cutter joins her, then Reeve. The melodic humming rises into the night sky.

"Come on, goddamn crazies. Humming isn't going to win this race," Cashal says as he surfs away.

Camas smiles at Reeve and Cutter. They take a quick drink from their water bottles, then hop on their boards and surf on down the dune.

A wall of sand hums loudly with a full sky of glowing Milky Way stars overhead. Kangaroo-like hopping rodents match the beat of the Bluey's music, jumping joyfully through the cold night air.

143

CHAPTER 35

TUMUCUMAQUE MOUNTAINS NATIONAL PARK, BRAZIL – 3,870,000 HA

(1.9631, -52.9463)

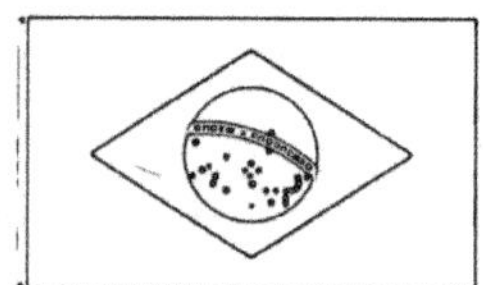

*P**arklands Enviro-Climate Challenge TV Graphic and Hare voiceover: Map of U.S. and a dot on all ten parks, Chaco's dot emphasized.*

"Chaco Culture National Historical Park is known as the hub of the Puebloan civilization and the ancestral homeland of numerous Southwestern tribes. The scale and sophistication of these communities and economies were unparalleled in the region where the Chacoan people expressed a complex solar and lunar cosmology in the form of their magnificent architecture. The park's iconic feature is Pueblo Bonito, an ancient structure of 600 to 800 rooms including thirty-five circular kivas, built in the years from 850 to 1150."

"Listen up," Cashal shouts. "Hare's calling!"

The Bluey's tap their phones in unison. Hare appears on racers' screens.

"Teams, I have some good news and some bad news."

"I'll just take the good news," Camas says hopefully, sitting on the edge of the trail.

"Shush."

"I'm not even near you."

Two cameramen film as Hare walks, phone in hand, standing in the center of the Great Kiva, a large circular stone structure in the ancient complex of Casa Rinconada.

"Some of you have made it to Chaco. Some of you will be getting here in the next several hours or days. When you arrive, you're halfway through the Parklands Enviro-Climate Challenge. Congratulations! The good news is that we're allowing you four extra hours of sleep here."

Camas, Reeve, and Cutter let out a whoop. Camas jumps up, and she and Cutter swing their right arms up into a high five slap.

"Listen up!" Cashal admonishes.

"You'll be getting your sleep at the top of a fifteen-foot star observatory tower."

The Blueys stare at their phones.

"Where is the tower, you may be wondering? That's the bad news. Your Chaco challenge is to build it. You'll build a platform using stone and beams, similar to what the Puebloans used to build these amazing structures twelve hundred years ago. We'll provide a plan and materials at the site. Your structure must be constructed with enough care for actual use by future park visitors. We'll supply a dome roof."

The Blueys look up at each other, eyebrows raised.

"You'll name one member of your team to use the paper and pen provided to map the night's sky, naming whatever constellations and stars he or she can recognize *without* the use of the sat phone. Fasten the star map as indicated on the plan."

"So much for sleep," Camas says.

Hare and the two cameramen run and jump into the heli-copter. The aircraft flies over the intricate walls of the ancient civilization.

"Keep it low. I hear there's a methane cloud the size of Delaware above us."

The pilot looks upward. "Christ."

Olivier Clan lectures to a room full of Harvard law students seated at wood desks in Austin Hall. Wood paneling and two centuries of oil-on-canvas robed law professors proctor behind him.

"That nearly concludes today's lecture."

The students begin sitting up in their seats. They straighten their papers and tap their phones inside purses and jackets, anxious to reunite with the pixel beachball bouncing around the concert of social society. They remain reserved, eyes on the professor.

"I have a reading that's not on the syllabus. I posted it just before class."

The students type on their laptops. Two take written notes.

"You will be asked to ratify the amendment in the reading as though you are a senator in the state assigned to you. Class adjourned."

Thomas and Sarah lie in a double sleeping bag under the night sky. Tents and protesters' rigs are scattered nearby under the moonlight.

"The stars are amazing," Sarah says in awe.

"I read that Chaco is an International Dark Sky Place."

"What's that?"

"It's kind of like a UNESCO World Heritage Site or a Biosphere Reserve, but instead of being recognized for its historical-cultural value, it celebrates the dark sky."

"It's beautiful. You're ruining it a bit with your headlamp," she teases.

Thomas reads from his phone. "It says that Chaco is under a 2,500 square mile methane hot spot that's affecting the health of the indigenous people. Seventy percent of the community lives within a half-mile of the oil and gas foot-print. Nausea, burning eyes, respiratory problems, and headaches are the reports from the community. Experts estimate that, conservatively, 5,000 cultural sites are completely unprotected. Gas flares light up the dark skies, and the leaking infrastructure of the oil and gas wells endanger the health of the Native American people who have lived here for centuries. *And* POTUS has proposed removing another 316,000 acres from protection."

"Oh no," Sarah squeezes Thomas's hand on top of the sleeping bag. "So much for sweet dreams."

Olivier stands at the front of the classroom. A slide on the screen behind him shows the vote.

"Five-eighths of you voted yay. Thirty-six percent nay. We needed sixty-seven percent to ratify."

"Mace Corning, representing the state of New York, you voted nay. Please explain."

"A green amendment could be an important symbol, but it's not practical. It may not change anything," says Mace.

"But even if it does, it could take decades for it to become meaningful."

A young woman with a short blond bob raises her hand.

"Caroline, from Delaware, you voted yay."

"Yes, sir. African Americans are three times more likely to die from exposure to small particle air pollution than the general population, according to a 2017 study published in the New England Journal of Medicine. I would ask my fellow senator Corning how saving lives is merely symbolic?"

"Mr. Corning?"

"The purpose of the green amendment is to reduce CO_2, and that burden should be placed on other areas of our economy."

"But, if..." Caroline stops herself.

"Proceed," Olivier waves her on.

"But, if every time a small indigenous community, or an urban community of color, rises to protect its environment and their right to clean air and water and is successful, and just a few years later, a large corporation with millions of dollars crush them and overturn the protections because of a change in political administration, there can never be progress to a greener world."

"It sounds like the rights would need to be irrevocable," Olivier writes on the whiteboard: *Natural Rights are the objects for the protection of which society is formed and municipal laws established. Thomas Jefferson to James Monroe, 1797.*

A young black woman with wire-rim glasses and a short Grace Jones crew cut wearing a T-shirt reading *Food Oasis, Not Food Desert* raises her hand.

"Yes, Ms. Cruciferous."

"The National Caucus of Environmental Legislature says that a Green Amendment to the Bill of Rights would hold officials accountable when their actions cause environmental harm because that would violate environmental constitutional rights including both present and future generations." She pauses. She opens her mouth, then closes it.

"Go on. You seem to have more to say."

"In response to Mr. Mace stating that it could take decades for the amendment to have an impact, I would point him to the 1948 United Nations Universal Declaration of Human Rights. Seven decades ago, few could have imagined the impact and that now the voices of the voiceless are amplified on an international level."

"Meaning?" Oliver asks.

"Meaning that even if it takes time to have full effect, the impact would be worth waiting for, sir."

Caroline raises her hand.

Olivier acknowledges her with a nod. "Caroline?"

"I think we need a constitutional convention."

"That's bold but unreasonable," Mace responds.

"There's only been one in the history of the constitution. Yes, it's a method to amend the constitution, but it's not used," Oliver says.

"An Article V convention could get all of the states together in one feel swoop." Caroline argues.

"Yes, Article V does potentially provide a way for the states to bypass congress, but it has never been used. How do you think it could happen now?" Oliver says.

Mace and some other students nod.

"Have you heard of Campaign for Cause?" Cruciferous asks.

"No."

"They're supporting young, diverse progressives to run for down-ballot races to build sustainable power in all fifty states."

"The kind of power that would eventually support a constitutional convention?" Olivier queries.

"Possibly," Caroline and Cruciferous say in unison.

"On a cold day in hell," Mace answers.

Stacey drives along a dusty road in Chaco with the production crew. Hare travels in a helicopter overhead. She comes around a corner, and an oil rig is driving fast in the center of the road. Stacey swerves to miss it.

"Christ, Stacey, are you OK?! I saw the wanker!"

"We're OK, thanks."

Hare sees a field of oil wells in the distance. He texts Thomas, *Drive through the ancient city, head northeast. You'll run straight into a drilling field.*

Thanks.

Sarah and the protesters join local Navajo tribe members at eight tall tanks with a vista of hundreds of oil drilling rigs behind. They hold a sign behind Sarah as she speaks to the camera. *Methane Gas, Odorless, Toxic, In Our Air.*

"The oil company here tells us the emissions are minimal. An anonymous friend lent us this infrared camera."

Sarah peers into the large camera then rushes to Thomas. She turns the infrared camera around so Thomas can film them. "Can you see it, everyone? Oh my God. It's just spewing from the pipes atop the tanks!"

Hare flies over the protesters as his cameraman films them below. The camera turns to film Hare.

"We have bad news that the Denver Dust Devils and the Hawaiian Heatwaves have dropped out for respiratory problems. A member on each team collapsed on the course. Local doctors told us they believe these athletes became ill from methane pollution created from oil drilling near Chaco and the nearby San Juan basin."

"Hare, the network called."

"Ratings are up from all the sat phone posts?"

"Yes, but you can't comment on the drilling rigs."

"Says who?"

"Some guy from BLM called. A Mr. Lonely."

"Tell Lonely, black lives do matter."

"Bureau of Land Management."

"I know what it stands for, Fonear."

"Hare, just cool it."

"I'm working on it, mate. I'm working on it."

CHAPTER 36
GOBI GURVANSAIKHAN NATIONAL PARK, MONGOLIA - 2,700,000 HA

(43.6648, 101.5248)

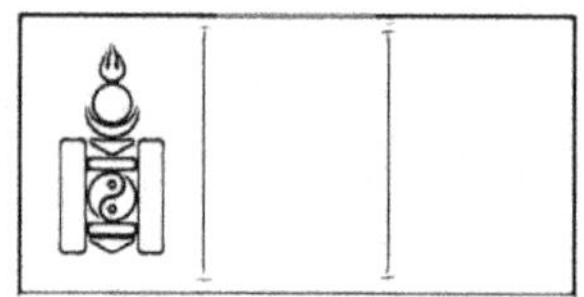

A rope encircles Camas and Cutter's waists as she pulls him along, his head bent down in exhaustion as they trudge through Chaco Canyon.

"Hang in there, Cutter," Camas says wearily.

"Camas, I can take over," Reeve calls out from the lead.

Camas wipes sweat from her freckled brow, her hair pasted to dirt-smudged temples.

"You're glowing, princess," Cashal teases.

"You've been carrying Cutter for two and a half miles," Reeve adds.

"I'm sorry I bonked," Cutter says weakly.

"I'm OK!" Camas says firmly. "Onward!"

Camas coughs and spits onto the ground. A race helicopter chops the air above. She squints upward to the sky. Tears fall from the corners of her eyes. She pulls her bandana down to wipe her eyes, then back up, and continues pulling Cutter.

"How in the world are you calling me?" Tilly asks.

"Hare gave me a phone."

"Who's Hare?"

"I'll explain later," Camas says weakly.

"OK, what's wrong? You sound exhausted."

"I am exhausted. I just needed to talk to you. Hear your voice. I don't know what the fuck I'm doing. I can't run anymore. I'm with a bunch of sweaty stinky guys, and I might stink more. I thought I was funny and cute. Seems I'm neither. I've been a bitch, and my formerly sexy outfits are covered in mud. I thought I was strong, but I don't know if I can make it through this."

"Oh, friend. I'm sorry."

"Don't be sorry. Give me some words of wisdom."

"That's why I'm sorry. I don't know what in the world I'm doing here either. It's hot as a sauna, and I thought I was a woman of color, but I'm the whitest one here. I thought I had some brains and some intuition about things. I thought I would understand why these countries weren't green, and all I can see is why these countries are at the tipping point for impending climate disasters. The oceans are rising into their coastal cities, the forests that protect them, and the animals in them are still being cut and killed for money. I usually have an idea or two, but I don't have anything. I feel smaller than a grain of sand in the Sahara. I feel worthless, helpless, and lost. I can't see a solution."

They are quiet.

"Well, fuck, sista. Thanks for being honest. I love you, and I wish I could help. At least you've taken my mind off of my silly televised Lord of the Flies ego-trip."

"Love you too and it's not silly at all. It's an epic adventure, and you're going to finish it. I wish I could help more," Tilly says warmly. "I can't help that your stinky, but one thing

I know is that you *are* strong enough. I know that. And that you're super cute too."

"Thank you. One thing I know about you is that you do have intuition. And that you may not be the same color as the people in Africa, but you are more compassionate than anyone I know, and you *do* know a life that's not as easy as the next person's, just like those people. I know that."

"Thanks, friend."

"I have to go. We're over halfway through the race. We're headed into the high desert."

"Thanks for the call. I really needed to hear your voice."

"Hey, I almost forgot. I took six seconds to glance at our email, and some United Nations dude is meeting you in Coat Dee Voyeur, or something like that."

"Ivory Coast, Cote d'Ivoire in French."

"I knew that." Camas checks her phone. "Here it is. His name is Kem Bullherder."

"Did he say how to contact him?"

"kbullherder@un.org and to meet him at La Pyramide in Abjidan 11:00 am tomorrow morning."

"OK, thanks. See you soon, sista."

"Not soon enough. When you think you don't know a solution, just remember what you've told me."

"What's that."

"Trust what you cannot see far more than what you see."

A middle-aged black man stands in front of a pyramid-shaped high rise, weathered and in severe disrepair. He wears a brown linen suit, light blue shirt, and well-worn tassel loafers.

"Hello, Mr. Bullherder?"

"Tilly? Nice to meet you. Call me Kem," he says warmly.

"Nice to meet you too." Tilly smiles. "This is Rongo."

"Hello! Welcome to Cote d'Ivoire."

Rongo shakes Kem's hand. "Cool building."

"Yes. La Pyramide was built during the Ivorian Miracle in the early 70s."

"I read about that," Tilly says. "Cote d'Ivoire had a lot of prosperity from coffee and cocoa."

"That's correct. They had the highest per capita income of all African countries, other than those with oil. Then the bottom fell out of the markets. Add to that a decade plus of civil war, and you have this. An old iconic monolith with deferred maintenance. It's a kindred spirit."

Tilly and Rongo look upward at the impressive structure.

"If a building could talk," Tilly says. She turns back to Kem. "May I ask why you wanted to meet with me?"

"I heard that you are visiting the countries with the greatest environmental problems. I also read about your organization One More Year. I wanted to find out more and make sure you got a proper tour of Cote d'Ivoire."

"Thank you," Rongo says. "What's your relationship to this country?"

"I study all places where environmental inequities take place. Especially racial inequities. I wrote a report for the United Nations about environmental conditions here."

"I'd like to learn whatever you can share," Tilly says.

"Rongo, where are you from?"

"I live in New Zealand, sir, but I am originally from Sierra Leone. I'm here to assist Tilly in her travels. Her husband is a close friend. I'm interested in your experiences too."

"Excellent. I took the liberty of calling a taxi for us. If you allow, I'll treat you to lunch in the French quarter in Grand Bassam."

"Oh, that sounds lovely, but we don't need anything too fancy," Tilly says.

"Alright then," Kem smiles as he opens the door of the taxi for Tilly. "We'll find just the right amount of fancy."

Reeve kneels on the architectural drawings of an astrological observation tower. He bends over to place his hands on the other side of the plan, sweat dripping onto the paper, and calls out instructions. "Carefully mark out the ground using the wooden pegs, straight poles, and string provided!"

Camas and Cutter scurry to measure the ground. Cutter hammers a peg as Camas marks the spot.

"Dig the platform's holes and a hole in the center 400 by 400 millimeters and 250 to 400 millimeters deep."

"Slow down, buddy. It's hot, and we're slow," Camas yells.

"Sorry. Hey, Camas, let's trade places."

"No, you hold table pose, my guru. I'm OK. Go on."

"I'll help dig the pier holes with you."

"They only gave us two shovels. We'll take turns," Camas answers.

"They gave us the cement piers. Couldn't they have dug the holes too?' Cutter complains as digs.

"No kiddin'," Cashal agrees. He stands over Reeve, looking at the plan.

"Grab the measuring tape and twine and start helping, Hobbit-hole!" Camas calls.

"Tolkien is from England, not bonnie Scotland."

"Do they build things in Scotland, or just boss blokes around?"

Cashal picks up the tools and saunters to the building site. "It's hotter than hades."

Camas lies on her stomach with her forearms resting on the plan. "You should first loosely erect the posts and make adjustments before securing them!" Camas reads.

"There are eight posts and four of us. How do we do that?" Cutter asks.

"It says to use an off-cut of wood bolted to the central column to measure from."

"They precut everything. There aren't any off-cuts."

"Can we just use some twine?" Camas suggests.

"This is going to take us all bloody day!" Cashal shouts.

Cutter hammers a piece of wood to hold the twine. "Aaaaaargh. Dammit!"

The Blueys sleep peacefully under the starry night sky above the desert on the floor of the observatory.

Reeve wakes the Blueys under the dark sky. They roll up their mats and pull out energy bars for a breakfast. Cashal and Cutter look at the Chaco race map.

"If I eat one more cardboard breakfast, I'll kill myself," Cashal complains.

Camas pulls a bar out of her pack and pokes it out towards him.

"Funny," Cashal says dryly.

"I'd kill for a Heaven's Brothers drip right now," Cutter says as he drinks from his water bottle.

"Nice work on the star map, Reeve," Camas says, shining her phone flashlight on the map nailed to a post at eye level.

"Thanks, Camas. I think I got most of them. I earned the astronomy merit badge in Boy Scouts."

Reeve and Camas sit down on the tower's edge and look out over the dark canyon. The sound of a hammer banging on wood is heard faintly in the distance.

"Nice. Hey, have you called your wife with your new phone?"

"No. She's not expecting a call."

"Josh isn't either, but I can't keep wondering if he's met someone else. Some other girl."

"This race gives us a lot of time to think, that's for sure."

"I wish I could just check his phone when I get back, but that's crazy snooping."

"Pretty much."

"Ugh."

"I had a friend who told me he snooped on his wife. I asked, 'What about trust?' He said, 'This isn't about trust. It's about self-interest and verifying self-interest.' I reminded him that he was just repeating what the President said about Russia."

"What did he say?"

"He just shrugged it off."

Camas takes a bite of her protein bar. She is quiet for a few moments. "I don't want to be the kind of person who shrugs."

"What do you mean?" Reeve asks.

Camas turns around to see where Cashal is. Cashal is loading his pack. Camas whispers, "I guess that's the problem. Love can't be about self-interest. So if I only care about myself and don't have trust, I can't have love."

Reeve smiles. "Sounds like you want both."

"Come on, Blueys! Get off your lazy arses, and let's make tracks!" Cashal calls.

The tired racers scramble to gather their meager belongings. They quickly dress wounds, smear sunscreen on their faces, and stuff their packs.

Camas notices two extra pieces of paper lying on the ground. She picks them up, folds them, and puts them in her pack.

The team climbs down the tower. In the distance, the moonlight reveals silhouettes of observatory towers in various stages of construction.

The Bluey's run with headlamps along a trail through the desert canyon.

"Cutter and Reeve, the medallion should be inside that round building," Cashal says, pointing. "Camas and I will meet you over there at the visitor building."

"All for one, remember?" Camas says, walking towards Reeve.

"Why should we all go the extra distance?"

"That's the race premise, captain tartan, and I don't want to be alone with your fart bombs."

Cutter laughs.

The four athletes hike to the circular stone kiva of Casa Rinconada. They find the medallions stacked in the center of the open-air structure.

Cashal counts the medallions. "Four are taken. I thought we'd be in a stronger position."

"That's better than twentieth," Cutter responds.

"A lot better," Reeve says.

"Let's do it."

"Four parks to go," Camas says wearily.

"You're doing great, Camas," Reeve says.

Camas smiles. She puts her hand on the stack of medallions. The others follow.

"On three. One two..."

"Brave Blueys!" they call out together.

"Ouch, my finger!" Cutter yells.

CHAPTER 37
BJESHKËT E NEMUNA NATIONAL PARK, KOSOVO - 63,028 HA
(43.6234, 20.1879)

Tilly looks out the window of the taxi at a row of French colonial ghost mansions. African fig tree vines wander across the masonry walls of the grimy structures.

"These weathered buildings are eery and elegant at the same time."

"Many of these buildings were built at the end of the 19th century. Mother nature is having her way. The city is a UNESCO heritage site, so hopefully, some restorations will occur over the coming years."

The taxi drives quickly through the quaint old town and pulls in front of a small café bustling with a collection of Ivorians and tourists. The walls are painted a deep blue covered with colorful modern paintings, straw hat-shaped hanging lights, and a Matisse-like mural reading *La Case Bleue*. The abstract images seem to come to life under the zougoulu beat.

"Spaghetti a la crème du truffe," Tilly orders in her best French accent.

"I'll have the sole meuniere, si vous plais," Rongo adds.

"Et monsieur?"

"Cote d' Porc, merci."

"Bon choix," the waiter responds. "I will be back with your drinks."

"Well, Mademoiselle De Montagne, c'est trop chic?" Kem asks Tilly.

"It's perfect. Paris in the tropics."

Rongo and Kem laugh. The waiter returns with two kir royales and a Chill Citron beer for Rongo.

"You know about the Ivorian Miracle. Do you know of the Ivorian Debacle?"

"The toxic spill?" Rongo asks.

"Yes."

"Please tell us," Tilly requests.

"In 2006, a large ship dumped about ten swimmings pools worth of uber toxic waste in twelve places throughout Abjidan."

"Oh my. What in the world was the waste?" Tilly asks.

"The ship produced naphtia onboard, a byproduct of gasoline coker, which earned them about 20 million in profit. The nasty waste was the slops from the caustic washing to make the naphtia."

"Shit."

"Mierde," the waiter says as he puts down their food. "My uncle died in the tragedy, and my cousin has had three miscarriages."

"Oh, I'm so sorry," Tilly says, looking him in the eye.

"May I bring you anything else?"

"No, thank you," Rongo says.

"The ship chartered by Desfigura, a 150 billion dollar multinational energy and metals trading company with connections throughout Europe and Asia, tried to offload the stuff in the Port of Amsterdam. About midway through transferring the slops, the port officials raised the price 3,700 percent because people complained of the horrific odor right away. The ship balked at the new price and was allowed to pump the muck back onto the vessel."

"Is that allowed?"

"No, it's not."

Tilly and Rongo are transfixed.

"Desfigura tried to get Nigeria to take the slops, but they refused, so the ship made its way to Abjidan. Immediately, people knew something was terribly wrong. They even tried to block the trucks bringing the waste into the dumpsites, which took about two weeks to accomplish. They dumped two tons of hydrogen sulfide, which, as you may know, is highly toxic and hangs close to the ground because it is heavier than air. You can detect it as rotten egg smell at first, but it quickly deadens the sense of smell, so it goes on to kill and injure without people being aware. Seventeen people died, and 30,000 to 100,000 injured."

Rogo pushes his plate away a few inches.

"Everything OK?" Kem asks.

"I've lost my appetite a bit, I'm afraid," Rongo responds.

"I'm sorry."

"It's OK," Rongo says. "Please continue."

"Why in the world did the Abjidan port allow it?" Tilly asks.

The civil war was going on, which created chaos and corruption. During the voyage between the Netherlands and Cote d'Ivoire, a new Ivorian company was created to distribute the waste around the city. Many officials resigned afterward, including the Prime Minister."

"Have the people been paid for the catastrophe?" Rongo asks.

"Desfigura settled, and the victims got a little over $1,000 each. Part of the retribution got siphoned off into some mystery company in the process."

"Oh, my goddess," Tilly says woefully. "We act as though a monetary payment repays death and destruction of life and nature." Tilly's voice raises. "Instead of retribution, there should be incarceration and forced liquidation of the offender."

"The city plans to cover one of the dumpsites with an urban park. I'm here to make sure they do it safely."

"I know a mushroom expert. Maybe he could help them do more clean-up before they cover it? It might make it safer." Tilly offers.

"Interesting. Yes, please send me the name."

"I will. Thank you for lunch and your time, Kem."

"You're welcome. Where next?"

"I'm going to Afghanistan and Myanmar. Rongo's heading home."

"Safe travels, both of you. Tilly, be careful. Well, you know about Afganastan, and I hear there's also unrest in Burma."

"I will. What's next for you after Abjidan?"

"I'm headed to the U.S. to attend the National People of Color Environmental Leadership Summit."

"That sounds important," Rongo says.

Tilly nods.

"It will be. Sadly, it's not the first. The first was in Washington DC in 1991, thirty years ago. We established a set of environmental justice principles."

"Like what?" Tilly asks.

"There were seventeen principles. Everything from the micro of asking individuals to make choices to consume as little of Mother Earth's resources as possible..."

Tilly interrupts. "Micro but macro-important. That's what One More Year is all about. Asking people to keep their stuff longer and buy less stuff. Sorry to interrupt."

Kem smiles. "It's a noble movement, indeed." He continues, "...to affirming the sacredness of Mother Earth, ecological unity and the interdependence of all species, and the right to be free from ecological destruction, to universal protection from nuclear testing and toxic wastes that threaten the fundamental right to clean air, land, water, and food."

"Where's the conference?" Tilly asks.

"Las Vegas."

Tilly's eyebrows raise.

"Ironic, I know."

Tilly rests her hand on Kem's arm. "Time is not a forward-going arrow as we've been told. Without time, you won't be late. Thirty years ago or now."

"This could be the one that turns the tide," Rongo adds reverently.

"You are wise young people. Can I do anything for you?"

"Oh, no. Thank..." Tilly stops herself. "Well, there is one thing. You know the mudslide in Liberia?"

"I do."

"There's a treasure chest of diamonds in the city government's bank. Can you see if you can wrestle those loose to help the people they were intended to help?"

"I heard a rumor of that. I'll see what I can do."

"Thank you."

Rongo shakes Kem's hand. Kem kisses Tilly on the cheek.

"Are you sure you're going to be OK by yourself in Afghanistan?" Rongo says.

Tilly and Rongo stand on the sidewalk outside the Félix Houphouët Boigny International Airport.

"Yes, I'll be fine." Tilly pauses. "You know that I was skeptical when you first met me in Liberia."

"That's putting it mildly."

"But I'm so grateful for your help. I know Liam would prefer you come with me, but I just have a couple more stops, and I promised him I'd find guides there."

"I'm happy you decided to fly."

"That helped him feel better too. I'll be home sooner."

"I hope to see you and Liam in New Zealand."

"That would be lovely. Please thank Samba for me. I hope to meet her too when we visit."

"One more time?" Rongo asks as he crouches with legs bent and hands at his sides, palms outward.

"Is this cultural misappropriation if I do it here in public?"

Travelers walk quickly to their flights.

"You, Tilly, Native American woman of color, must know the answer to that?"

Tilly pauses, thinking. "I join you and request the grace of your ancestor Maori chief, Te Rauparaha. I join you to stand up for those who can't stand up for themselves."

"Yes," Rongo bows his head.

Tilly sets down her backpack and stands shoulder to shoulder with Rongo with slightly bent knees.

They begin making loud guttural noises, their hands vibrating near their hips, arms curved. With strong rhythmic voices, they slap their thighs, chest and swing their arms in fists to the works of an ancient haka. In unison, "Ka mate! Ka mate! Ka ora! Ka ora! Ka mate! Ka mate! Ka ora! Ka ora!"

People stop to watch the two friends in powerful haka farewell.

"Tenei te tangata, pu-huru-hur, nana nei I tiki mei, whakawhiti te ra! Upane! Kaupane! Hupane! Kaupane! Whiti te ra! Hi!"

They pause and take a few moments of silence.

"Be safe, my strong sister Tilly."

"You too, brother Rongo."

The two embrace. Tilly picks up her pack and walks into the airport.

Tilly texts Camas, *There's a people of color environmental justice conference in Vegas next week. Some green big wigs, I think. Sarah probably knows but wanted you to know too, for what it's worth. Stay safe and strong.*

CHAPTER 38
PLITVICE LAKES NATIONAL PARK, CROATIA – 29,690 HA

(44.8654, 15.5820)

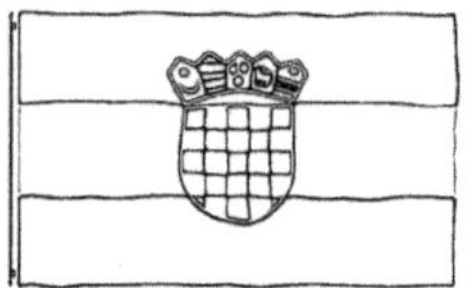

Viewers across the country and globe watch fast-paced, grainy, social media music ToeSock clips of Parklands Enviro-Climate Challenge athletes in victory, weariness, pain, and defeat.

Background music: Pink Sweats, At My Worst, "I want someone who'll love me at my worst."

Bo Milpitas of the Silicon Squalls rubs his sore balls. "Get the hell out of here, Franklin!"

"That mountain bike get the best of ya'?" Franklin responds.

Background music: Ashnikko, Slumber Party featuring Princess Nokia, "Slumber party."

. . .

Camas's head is down practicing tying knots in the dark at the top of the observation tower. The stars fill the sky behind her. Her phone flashlight illuminates the rope. She looks up. "Cutter, cutie, why are you filming me?"

"We didn't get any action shots today."

"This isn't action, and you should be sleeping. We only get three hours."

"No, but it's real."

"Go to sleep, buddy."

Cutter lies down on his sleeping pad. "Sweet dreams, Camas."

"Shut the hell up!" Cashal yells in the background.

Background music: Trevor Daniel, Falling, "My last made me feel I would never try again, but when I saw you, I felt something I never felt."

"Don't fall out, sweet Sarah!"

"I won't!"

The CJ5 Camper travels down the road. Sarah opens the back door of the camper and films the Blenheim Blizzards on motorbikes followed by the activist convoy.

"The Blenhein Blizzards lead the Parklands Enviro-Climate Challenge as they ride on motorbikes the 250 miles from Chaco to Mesa Verde," she says into the camera then points the camera back to the road. A vehicle in line pulls out to pass the Blizzards. It is a passenger van with the Denver Dust Devils and the Hawaiian Heatwaves wearing gas masks.

Background music: Lil Dicky, Earth, "We love the earth. It is our planet. We love the earth. It is our home."

"Ranger Joe Sweeney here at Mesa Verde. Follow @mesaverdenps, and don't forget to let your state representatives know that our outdoor recreation economy is at risk. Our 5,000 archaeological sites, including 600 cliff dwellings, are showing the effects of climate. I'm here at Spruce Tree House, where these climate changes have caused sections of the rock to cleave from the face."

He covers his head and ducks as he looks overhead at an imaginary falling rock for effect.

Background music: Natalie Taylor, Surrender, "Whenever you're ready."

The Supercell Swedes climb Crestone Needle. Eva Visby's face is tense as she looks down. Her teammate Elias films her from below. She hesitates on the rock face as Lucas waves her on to continue.

Background music: Post Malone and Swae Lee, Sunflower, "Then you're left in the dust unless I stuck by ya."

. . .

Camas rides a dirt trail on her mountain bike. She turns a corner and narrowly avoids a mud hole. She jumps off the bike, pulls out her camera, and waits.

Cashal comes around the corner fast, and his bike slides as he falls face down in the mud. He stands up and wipes the mud from his face, then sees Camas filming and makes a guttural animal cry to the sky, "Aaaaaaaaarghhhh!"

Background music: Brent Faiyaz, The Creatur, "Don't act like I'm average."

Sarah hikes a steep mountainous trail. She arrives at the top, panting, and walks to the edge of the overlook.

Background music: Kid Cudi vs. Crookers, Day 'n' Night, "Day 'n' night."

Short day and night clips of the weary, dust-covered, Canadian Cyclones hiking through the red rock desert and plateaus.

Background music: Surf Mesa featuring Emilee, ily (I love you), "I love you, baby, and if it's quite alright, I need you, baby."

. . .

The Tokyo Tsunamis hike the sand dunes. Flora Shiko-saki has her arm around Ren Kyush as he limps up the hill. At the top of the hill, they stop to rest, and Ren opens up the bandage rap on his leg, revealing a sore oozing with pus. Jiggling video footage of the team putting on sandsurf boards. Ren sits on his board, pulled by two of her team members. The board hits a clump of grass, and he flies face-first into the sand.

Background music: Big Home Ty.Ni, Jelly, "Watch my ass cheeks shake like jelly."

Camas pounds the last nail into the observation tower at the bottom of the steps.

"Whoop!" she calls. "Finished Bluey's. Let's chow!"

"Test it out, Camas!" Cutter yells.

Camas starts up the stairs.

"Come on. Give it some swagger!" Cashal calls out.

Camas shakes her booty up the stairs and dances at the top.

Background music: Fat Joe, Remy Ma featuring French Montana, Infared, All the Way Up, "Go all the way up. Go all the way up."

The Blueys hike to the foot of Square Tower in Hovenweep. Reeve films Cutter, Cashal, and Camas staring up at the three-story ancient tower.

Background music: Say So, Doja Cat, "Didn't even notice, no punches left to roll with. You got to keep me focused. You want it, say so."

A very bumpy video closeup with beads of water on the screen. The Queensland Compasses bump up and down in the whitewater rapids. Suddenly, the camera faces the sky as the raft bumps the athlete out of the raft and downstream.

Background music: Lady Gaga, Paparazzi, "I'm your biggest fan. I'll follow you until you love me."

Canyonlands Ranger Karen Harker films a herd of desert Big Horn Sheep at sunset at the stunning Mesa Arch. "Canyonlands and nearby Arches National Park bring over 2.4 visitors who spent $246 million in our communities. What was the number of days that the people in these communities were allowed to review environmental reports for the oil and gas leases covering 134,000 acres near the parks?"

Ranger Harker pauses to take a panorama of the breathtaking scenery of the colorful canyon and its dramatic rock formations, then turns the camera back on herself.

"Zero. Zero days."

Background music: Justin Timberlake featuring Timbaland, Sexy Back, "I'm bringing sexy back."

. . .

Camas walks in a slow-motion video in her sports bra arm in arm with shirtless Cutter and Reeve down a rugged desert trail. Sweat glistens on their bodies. Their eyes search intently, faces scratch and smudged with dirt. They begin to run, straining, past Cashal, and dive into a wide river.

Background music: Rex Orange County, It's Not the Same Any More, "It's not the same anymore. I lost the joy in my face."

"Some hippie chick is posting videos of the race leaders. She wears a gas mask!" Fremont says to Hare on the phone.

"And?"

"And she's scooping some of our cameramen."

"She's got a big following. I can't imagine it's hurting ratings."

"The ratings are up with all of the social postings by the racers."

"That's good, isn't it?"

"She's reciting environmental mumbo jumbo too. And she's got the rangers participating."

"Text me a link."

Hare hangs up. He looks at his phone. He taps to a photo of Felice, Jamie, Buck, and Garfield.

CHAPTER 39
BUMDELING WILDLIFE
SANCTUARY, BHUTAN – 152,061 HA

(27.8236, 91.4435)

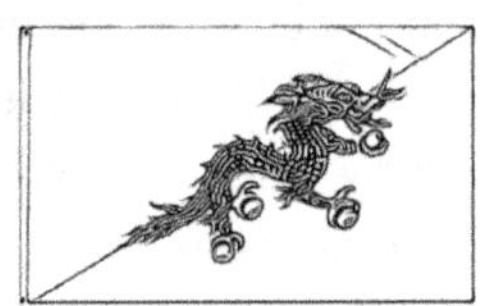

Tilly visits the Buddhas of Bamiyan, 100-foot 3-D light-show-created buddhas recreating the fourteen-century-old stone Buddhas destroyed by the Taliban.

Tilly wears a long sleeve green dress over light blue cotton pants and a hijab over her head, around her neck, and over her shoulder as she walks through the Ka Faroshi bird market in Kabul with the Minister of the Environment. Yellow canaries in colorful cages hang on a shop wall. Roosters, chukar partridges, pigeons, finches, and larks hop about in wicker cages and metal aviaries.

"People find the birds bring peace to their homes in these times of war," the minister says.

Coos of pigeons and the bouncy, rhythmic chuck of chukars fill the air.

"How do these birds survive the air pollution? I read that it's the fourth-worst in the world."

"Yes, our pollution has killed more people than the wars themselves. In the mid-eighties in Mexico City, pollution caused birds to fall out of the sky. I have to admit that I wonder how many of the canaries here could make a flight in our air."

"Canaries in a coal mine," Tilly responds.

The minister nods.

"Why is the environment so degraded?" Tilly asks.

"We have been in war for four decades. It's nearly impossible to make any headway when we are just trying to survive. We're also one of the most vulnerable countries to climate change, and all of the things that it has brought will only get worse --drought, floods, avalanches, extreme weather events, conflict, and mass displacement."

"Is there an end in sight for the war?"

"Casualties last year were lower, but the UN estimates that eighty percent of the conflicts here are over land, water, and resources, so it is difficult to see the end."

Tilly looks worried. She walks through the busy market. "Just think if the United States had focused its two trillion dollars on climate and infrastructure rather than the war effort."

"There have been a few bright spots."

"I'd love to know about those."

"We've received support from the World Bank and others to grow saffron. Farmers can earn seven times more than growing poppies for opium. Women account for about eighty percent of the production and hold most of the knowledge about the drying and refining."

"How wonderful."

"Yes, it's a small positive change, but it's not insignificant. I'll see if I can set up a tour. I wouldn't want you to leave without some hope."

"Thank you so much for meeting with me, Minister." Tilly

puts her hand on her heart and bows her head. "I always have hope."

In the early morning, Tilly walks along the edge of a field with lavender saffron flowers. Women dressed in long beige tunics and lavender scarves over their heads bend down, pluck flowers, and place them in a basket. The Afghan women work sitting around a long table with large piles of saffron flowers. They carefully pull off the precious bright red stigmas and place them in a white bowl in the center of the table.

CHAPTER 40
LOS GLACIARES NATIONAL PARK, ARGENTINA, 726,927 HA

(-50.3306, -73.2342)

Parklands Enviro-Climate Challenge TV Graphic and Hare voiceover: Map of U.S. with a dot on all ten parks, Mesa Verde's dot emphasized.

"Mesa Verde National Park is home to some of the most well-known and well-preserved Ancestral Puebloan archaeological sites. About 5,000 of these sites exist, including 600 cliff dwellings. The park's iconic feature is Cliff Palace, the largest cliff dwelling in North America and a magnificent structure of 150 rooms and 23 kivas."

"You'll build a traditional dog travois which you'll pull from the Mesa Verde entrance to the cave dwellings with your gear on top. You'll encounter Spruce Tree House caves about 25 miles from the entrance and can sleep in any of them as long as you spend at least four hours camped. This forced rest is to allow some teams to gain some ground and because most of you look like death warmed over, and we're hoping to keep you alive through the rest of the race."

"I can't believe we're being forced to rest at the caves," Cashal says, trudging behind Cutter and Reeve.

"Geez, man, I could use a four-hour rest," Reeve says. "Camas, my turn with the dog sled."

"Thanks, Reeve. I'm OK for a bit longer."

"From my calculations, we're just a couple hours behind the Blizzards and four in front of the Toros. We'll keep going," Cashal says.

"It's a rule, not a suggestion. Let's just get there," Camas says wearily.

"Don't drop my pack, bitch."

"What did you say?" Camas scowls.

"A bitch is a dog. It's a dog sled. I'll call Cutter a bitch too when he pulls that sled."

"If I didn't have this thing strapped to me, your hard-boiled Scotch eggs would be deep-fried inside your sausage and hung high on these teepee poles."

"Easy friends. We're just eleven miles to the caves. Hang in there. Hey, Camas, I'll pull the travois. You're awesome."

Camas helps Reeve strap the A-shape pole dog sled around his hips. The apex of the A is wrapped in leather to ineffectively ease friction, and its splayed ends drag on the ground.

Reeve takes a few strong steps with the travois. "Poor Puebloan dogs."

"No shit," Camas says, running to the front of the group, spitting on Cashal as she passes.

Reeve, Cutter, Cashal, and Camas sit on the ledges of their respective caves, looking out over the canyon under a starlit sky. They eat jerky, dried fruit, nuts and sip from water bottles. Camas wipes her face with some of the water and the sleeve of her shirt. One by one, Reeve, Cutter, and Cashal lie down on their sleeping pads. Exhaustion tugs their eyes closed instantaneously.

Camas leans out from her cave and sees no dangling legs. "Good night, Blueys," she calls.

No answer.

Camas walks on blister-covered bare feet to her pack, pulls out the two pieces of paper, and sits back down. She folds the first piece of paper like an accordion lengthwise in four folds, then repeats four folds on the opposite side. She unfolds it and counts twenty-five squares. She carefully uses her dirty fingernails to reinforce the creases and weaken the fibers. She holds the paper between her two hands and slowly, silently, tears it. She repeats with the second piece of paper, then carefully writes on each of the fifty pieces. She puts the rectangular paper pieces into the ziplock baggie she had brought to carry her one makeup essential, auburn-bronze eyeliner, which hasn't seen the light of day. She uses the liner to write *Take One!* in thick letters on the outside of the plastic bag, then puts the baggie in her pack. She lies down to sleep.

Parklands Enviro-Climate Challenge TV Graphic and Hare voice-over: Map of U.S. with dots on all ten parks, Hovenweep's dot emphasized.

"Hovenweep National Monument protects six prehistoric Pueblo villages, all noted for their towers in an expanse of mesa tops. The park's iconic feature is Square Tower, a three-story ancient Puebloan ceremonial structure built on top of a boulder at the head of Little Ruin Canyon."

The Blueys watch Hare on their sat phones.

"You'll mountain bike the eighty-mile out-and-back route of the Navajo-Hovenweep Utah Classic, where you'll stop mid-way to hike the Square Tower trail and retrieve a medallion."

Dust covers the Blueys, and the desert heat bears down as they ride the rolling terrain, rising slowly in elevation along barren rocky trails.

"How can this be so hard? Mountain biking is our sport," Camas whines.

"Because we're on mile 557 of the race," Reeve says, breathing hard.

"And that doesn't include the 1,748 miles our arses have been bouncin' around on the motos," Cashal adds.

Camas turns a corner and pulls over on the ridge of a hill overlooking the flat high sagebrush desert of Cajon Mesa with the Sleeping Ute Mountain in the distance. Reeve, Cutter, and Cashal pull up next to her.

Cashal looks down at the map. The medallion should be inside that huge boulder down there," he says, pointing down the hill.

"Is that a house?" Cutter asks.

"Aye. Boulder House, it says."

"Looks like a quarter-mile. I'll get it!" Camas calls out, jumping on her bike. "You guys take a rest. I'll be right back with it."

Cashal looks up, surprised. "Hey, Red! Wait up. We're in this with ya."

"No, no," Camas shouts. "I'm good." She rides off.

"Hell you are. Let's go, guys." Cashal follows Camas.

Cutter and Reeve look at each other and smile. They hop on their bikes and follow Cashal up the trail. The Blueys come upon a massive boulder with rooms carved inside like a cave with stacked rock columns for support. Alongside its crumbling walls are golden chamisa, spiky yucca, and flowering cliffrose. The Blueys see the stacked medallions glowing from sunlight streaming through the mouth of the boulder cave.

"This building looks like a mountain lion head that might eat me," Cutter says, looking up at the curved roof of the structure.

"Come along, wimpy pants. It's a ritual," Cashal says as he marches inside.

"Aren't you the softy, Cash," Reeve teases as they lay their hands one by one on top of the stack.

"Don't want to jinx us now! Ready now? One two three..."

"Brave Blueys!" they join in as they raise the medallion off the stack.

Reeve puts the medallion in his pack. He counts the stack. "You're right, Cash. Looks like we're in second place."

"Right on, Blueys," Camas says, giving each a high five. "Hey, you guys head back. I'm going to take a piss, and I'll catch you."

The guys walk out of Boulder House, get back on their mountain bikes and start the ride back.

Camas crouches down to pee. She stands up, pulls up her shorts, and opens her pack. She looks out of the cave. No race cameras in sight, she pulls out the baggy with pieces of paper along with a rubber hair tie and a five-inch ball bungee cord. She pulls out her pocket knife and cuts a one-half-inch slit in the top of the bag under the zipper. She carefully threads the hair tie into the hole and loops the other end through, then puts one of the ball ends of the bungee through the hair tie. She wraps the bungee and bag on top of the stack of medallions and secures the balls. She moves the bag, so the words *Take One* are clearly in sight.

Camas runs out of the stone womb, jumps onto her bike, and races to catch the Blueys, who laugh and joke as they ride with vigor in a quest to overtake the Blizzards.

Parklands Enviro-Climate Challenge TV Graphic and Hare voice-over: Map of U.S. with a dot on all ten parks, Canyonland's dot emphasized.

"Canyonlands National Park is known for its dramatic desert landscape carved by the Colorado and Green rivers with fantastically formed buttes, arches, fins, and spires. The park's iconic feature is Mesa Arch, a majestic vista of White Rim country and the La Sal Mountains, on the edge of a 500-foot cliff, part of a 1,200-foot drop into Buck Canyon.

"You've been scorched for days, and you'll be human hotdogs on the barbie soon at the grand finale, so you'll have a green respite on the Green River, mermaids."

"The other shoe?" Camas says, waiting.

"Shush!" Cashal says.

"But, of course, even though it will be cooler and green, it won't be easy."

Camas sighs. Cutter puts his arm around her sweaty shoulder.

"You'll start slow and peaceful with a nice fifteen-mile swim. Only your packs will have a flotation device. Next, you'll find a four-man raft..."

"Hey! Four-person!" Camas says.

"Shush!"

"...at The Confluence and spill down Cataract Canyon in world-class whitewater. If you make it down the river, I'll see you at the Grand Canyon."

"Damn. I've trained with Tilly on long swims but fifteen miles?"

"We'll take it easy, Camas," Reeve assures her.

"The hell we will. We've got to catch the Blizzards."

Camas taps her phone, taps it again.

"And what the hell are you doing on that phone all the time?"

Camas shoves the phone into her pack.

"How's it going, sweetie?" Felice asks as she runs along the perimeter on the high plateau of their island, the waves crashing far below.

"It's a mess."

"I've been watching. Except for that kookie group of doomsayers, the teams are doing great. I called Fremont yesterday trying to find you, and he said ratings are up from racers' videos."

"Fuck the ratings."

"Hare. What's wrong?"

"I'm sorry. I realized that I've been escaping reality."

"You're the originator of the reality show. How are you escaping it?"

"I've been traipsing around the world with the lens pointed to the world's most beautiful places. Well, you know, the lens is just that. A narrow view, and if you turn the camera in any other direction, there's pollution and poverty. The water's dirty from mine runoff. The air's killing folks from fossil fuels. Add a bit of radioactive waste for good measure!"

Felice stops running as she arrives at their stone house. She looks across the Tasman Sea from the backyard to the tall, cathedral-like, dolerite sea cliffs of the neighboring cape, the hexagonal prisms offering a prayer to the hopeful sea.

"I don't see pollution and poverty."

"Exactly. Not only do I film a bubble of eco beauty, but I've put you and the boys in my bubble too."

"I like our bubble."

"So do I, but I just can't pretend that this planet's going to survive in the status quo. It's not just America. You've seen those open-pit coal mines we've flown over at home. They say 50,000 mines have been abandoned or not properly rehabilitated in Australia, polluting waterways or in danger of collapsing. I've been flying over these magnificent parks where ancient civilizations constructed intricate multi-story towers overlooking the colorful canyons with sophisticated solar calendars and archeoastronomy legacies."

"That sounds amazing, my love."

Hare gets louder. "Did you know that archaeologists have only surveyed two percent of the newly leased oil and gas land over here? Two percent! Who knows what other treasures are under there?"

"What can you do about it? You're just one person."

Hare looks down at Sarah and Thomas's car convoy on the highway below.

"I'm not sure."

LAGUNA DEL TIGRE NATIONAL PARK, GUATEMALA – 337,899 HA

(17.5730, -90.6773)

Parklands Enviro-Climate Challenge TV Graphic and Hare *voiceover: Map of U.S. with a dot on all ten parks, Grand Canyon's dot emphasized.*

"Grand Canyon National Park is home to the one-mile deep and 277 river-mile long Grand Canyon, often included as one of the seven natural wonders of the world. Its jaw-dropping vistas make it nearly impossible to name a favorite. Still, if we must, one of the park's most iconic features is The Skywalk, a horseshoe-shaped steel frame with glass floor and windows that projects seventy feet from the canyon's west rim. This walk in the air, located on the tribal lands of the Hualapai Tribe, is visited by over one million people each year."

The Blueys ride motorbikes from Canyonlands towards the Grand Canyon. Tumbleweeds outnumber motorized travelers five to one.

"Still no word from Hare?" Camas asks over her helmet mic.

"He must be waiting to announce the Grand Canyon torture at the race camp," Cashal responds.

A group of chopper-style motorcycles and early model weathered trucks pass in the opposite direction. Three bike riders have beautiful olive-skinned faces, two with deep wrinkles. The three hold their left fists in the air as their motorized steeds gallop towards the sacred Clenched Fist Butte.

"Hey, look!" Camas says, pointing back at the caravan behind them.

A *Stop Uranium Mining Save the Grand Caynon* sign is tied to the back of a dusty orange Chevy truck.

"So what?" Cashal grunts.

"We've either seen no cars, or we've seen Teslas and Land Rovers on the way to some overpriced selfie river tour. Some of these things don't look like the others."

Camas sees Sarah pass by in the passenger seat of the CJ5 Camper.

"Sarah!" she shouts. "Wait! That's my friend Sarah. I'm following them! I'll meet you guys at base camp."

"Camas, we can't register without you," Reeve reminds her. "If we don't stay together, we'll be disqualified."

Camas slows to a stop. The others pull over too.

"Then come with me, please." She looks Reeve and Cutter in the eye. "Please."

Camas turns her bike around. Reeve and Cutter follow.

"You're fired!" Cashal shouts.

"You can't fire me! Come on, old man. Thirty-minute detour max!"

"Damn you, girlie. We're here to win, not sightsee!" Cashal turns his motorbike around, revs his engine, and follows.

The Blueys follow the tribal caravan onto a side road towards a majestic butte rising out of the middle of the desert. A large tent appears in the distance as the group rides through desert scrub of blackbrush, western honey mesquite, and sagebrush.

A television reporter films a group of Havasupai in colorful garments with men in bighorn sheep headdresses. Young girls hold baskets in their outstretched arms in a dance of grace, rhythm, and time.

Camas makes a quick right turn off the road into a parking field.

"Where the hell are we going?" Cashal asks.

"There's Sarah!"

"Who the hell is Sarah?"

"Wait here, Blueys. I promise it's important."

"Christ," Cashal grumbles.

Camas parks her bike. She takes off her helmet and puts it on her seat. She runs with a slight limp over to Sarah. They hug.

Reeve and Cutter walk towards the music tent as Cashal tinkers with his bike.

"Camas! It's so great to see you. Are you OK?" Sarah looks down at Camas's leg.

"Oh yeah. Just a fine combination of foot rot and bug bites. Nothing a good kick-ass desert adventure can't cure."

"Oh, I wish I could help you. Maybe we have something in our bag."

"We can't get outside help, but just seeing you is helping me. What is this shindig?"

Rhythmic drums sound in the background. A strong male voice addresses the crowd over a microphone. Reeve and Cutter walk up to see a small-framed man wearing an Arizona

Wildcats ballcap, singing in his native language of Yuman. His face balances peace and pain as he remembers the ancient words, his eyes closed.

"It's the Havasupai's annual protest at this sacred site trying to protect the Grand Canyon from the uranium mine."

"I thought it might be."

"Yeah, well, this time it's more urgent. Emerging Fusion, 'EF,' has applied to renew its permit, and the million-acre moratorium is stuck in the Senate. It seems if you take away liver failure and your skin falling off your body, nuclear is now..." Sarah makes air quotes. "...clean energy."

"Fuck that."

"Yeah, fuck that."

Thomas looks at Sarah, surprised. He kisses her on the cheek.

"Hey, Thomas!" Camas hugs Thomas.

"The mine could contaminate not only the world-renowned waterfalls but the health of forty million people downriver," Sarah says, passionately holding Camas's hand.

Thomas smiles. "These people could have cashed out with casinos and copters flight-seeing their falls. Instead, their legacy is truth, protecting mother earth with their ancient calls."

"I miss that warrior verse, brother." Camas hugs Thomas again.

"These people are the guardians of the Grand Canyon," Sarah says as she puts her arms around them both.

The Blueys pull into a large parking lot about six miles southeast of the resort town of Tusayan. They park their bikes and walk towards camp.

Hare and Stacey stand at the entrance to the camp.

"Welcome, Blueys," Hare says. He hands them a green envelope. "This is your map for your last park. Congratulations. You're in third place behind the Blenheim Blizzards and the Toro Tornados. The Welsch Wildfires and Missouri Climatrons are not far behind you. Don't waste your rest time. Trust me. You'll need it."

Camas walks through the gate past Hare. She looks him in the eye. "You call this a race. It's a fucking endurance death march."

"You're still alive. Hard to get you on camera Camas with all the f-bombs."

"Good to see you, Hare," Cashal says.

"Good work, Cashal."

"Kiss ass," Camas says under her breath as they make their way to the food station.

"I can't believe the Tornados passed us." Cashal shakes his head. "Must have been when you were sunbathing along the river."

"I don't remember applying my bronzing lotion as I was barfing on the shore." Camas sneers at Cashal. "And you were such a scaredy-cat on the water, you still have your life vest on."

"I'm savin' time. We're still in river country. Now, go get your grub and your Camas-plaining arse back asap to read Hare's canyon missive!" Cashal barks.

Camas walks wearily past a shower station, a food stall, and a set of crew tents to a group of porta-potties. A Red Heeler pup runs past her as she steps out of the toilet.

"Hey, little guy," she calls. She follows him a few steps, pets him, then notices a chain-link fence topped with three rows of barbed wire about 200 yards in the distance. She walks closer to look through the fence.

Camas takes a photo, then taps her phone.

"Camas. I just got the photo."

"Hi, Reina. We met some Havasupai tribal members at a protest today, and there's activity at Canyon Mine. Cheap TV bastards probably didn't want to pay tourist prices at Tusayan, so the race base camp is adjacent to the mine."

"Do you see anything else?"

"I'm looking in the fence, and I see two huge new tanks, the ones in the photo, some huge cannons shooting mystery spray into the air, and an enormous stack-of-cubes-scaffold-looking thinga-ma-gigger."

"Sounds like the headframe of the shaft. Bastards. They're moving forward before the permit's approved. I read in EF's 10-K filing they're maintaining the mine in standby mode. Christ, sounds like their standby mode is a four-point crouch at the block."

The two are quiet.

"Gotta get back before my team goes nuts looking for me."

"I know you do. Thanks for the recon. Be safe, Camas, and good luck finishing the race."

"I hope I can finish," Camas says, limping back to meet the Blueys.

The camera films a close-up of Hare looking through coin-operated steel binoculars overlooking the grandeur of the Grand Canyon. Hare steps away from the viewing scope to face the camera.

"Excitement! Excitement! Nine of the teams have made it to the grand finale park, the magnificent Grand Canyon. Thirteen have dropped out, and twenty-five are making their way here from Canyonlands with three stragglers still in Hovenweep."

The camera pans the majestic canyon view. The second camera films Hare framed by the wood and stone supports of the ancient stone lodge with colorful desert layers of the canyon behind.

"I'm here at historic 1914 Hermit's Rest on the south rim of the Grand Canyon. As we speak, the front racers are riding their motorbikes for the last stretch to Havasupai Hilltop. There they'll leave their motorbikes to hike eight miles down steep rocky trails in the extreme heat through the Havasupai tribe reservation and the most remote village in the lower 48, Supai. Continuing, they'll hike down more steep terrain through Havasu Canyon, past the waterfalls of dreams and postcards, nine miles to retrieve their last medallion and to the Colorado River. What next? The race crew will have delivered rafts just above the magical Confluence at river mile 157, where the desert sun radiates off the towering rock walls like a convection oven, and the turquoise waters of Havasu Creek meld with the red silt waters of the Colorado."

Thomas reads to Sarah from John Wesley Powell's 1869 journal, "We are now ready to start on our way down the Great Unknown. Our boats, tied to a common stake, chafe each other as they are tossed by the fretful river."

"The teams will raft the most dangerous and renowned rapids in the Colorado River, Lava Falls, the fastest navigable water in the Northern Hemisphere. There's a thirty-eight-foot drop, and the dangerous ride-of-their-lives will all take place in seconds! They continue the race for forty-six exhausting river miles past more than a dozen turbulent rapids, then take out at Diamond Creek Beach. On last legs, the racers will endure a soul-killing final nineteen-mile 3,400-foot elevation hike through the Hualapai Reservation and Peach Springs Canyon to the town of Peach Springs and the finish line!"

CHAPTER 42

CAIRNGORMS NATIONAL PARK, SCOTLAND – 452,800 HA

(57.0492, -3.5616)

The Blueys stumble over wet stones along the river shore, heads down in weary, delusional, irritable fatigue. Camas watches dragonflies float in the warm air over the edge of the stream, their silver-gauze wings beautifully veined with amber and ruby streaks.

"Wow, we're in prehistoric times with the dragonflies," Camas says slowly. "Look at their big eyes. Those eyes are 300 million years old. Even older than this canyon."

Reeve stops, opens his water bottle, and walks back to give her a drink. The Blueys hike on in silence as dragonflies weave in and out of their sagging bodies.

Sarah, Thomas, and Durga stand at the vertex of the Skywalk looking out over the pink, orange, and blue layers of sky and canyon.

Durga leans down to pick up her backpack. She pulls out a tattered Zane Grey paperback, opens it, and reads aloud. "He meant the Grand Canyon was only a mood of nature, a bold promise, a beautiful record. He meant that mountains had sifted away in its dust, yet the canyon was young. Man was nothing, so let him be humble. This cataclysm of the earth, this playground of a river was not inscrutable; it was only inevitable—as inevitable as nature herself. Millions of years in the bygone ages, it had lain serene under a half moon; it would bask silent under a rayless sun, in the onward edge of time. It taught simplicity, serenity, peace. The eye that saw only the strife, the war, the decay, the ruin, or only the glory and the tragedy, saw not all the truth. It spoke simply, though its words were grand: 'My spirit is the Spirit of Time, of Eternity, of God. Man is little, vain, vaunting. Listen. Tomorrow he shall be gone. Peace! Peace!'"

The three sigh in unison.

"Thanks, Mom," Sarah says.

"Simple peace serene...disconnection destruction...earth can not save man."

"Nice haiku." Sarah kisses Thomas.

Reeve walks strongly in the lead as Cashal squints at the map. He holds it close, then farther away, then close again.

"That's the route," Cashal says, pointing at a rock cairn alongside the waterfall. "I need to sit." Cashal sits and stares blankly at the stack of smooth stones.

"Is there a leprechaun hiding behind that cairn?" Camas teases in a slow brogue.

Cashal's speech is slurred. "Damn ye, lassie. It's a sith. Leprechauns are in Ireland."

"'Shee' what?"

"Sith, don't ya know?" Cashal speaks slowly. "Faery, still folk, pixies, the wee folk, prowlies, people of peace, the silent moving folk."

"We got it, we got it, captain fairy dust. A *she* it is. Here, drink this water," Camas says, kneeling on one knee, lifting her bottle to his lips. Cashal drinks slowly, then closes his eyes.

"Cutter, give him this energy chew." Reeve grimaces with worry.

Cutter walks over to Cashal, taps him on the shoulder. Cashal opens his eyes. Cutter grabs his hand, pulls his pack off, and puts it over his own. "Eat this, Cash! Let's go, man. It's the last park. You got this!"

Reeve takes the lead and Camas the rear as the Blueys descend the steep rocky path. They hear the loud crash of water in the distance.

As they move down over the rocks, Cutter keeps Cashal close, giving him instructions. "There's a good hold here, man. Grab that root, there."

Reeve steps down onto a ledge near the top of a two-hundred-foot waterfall. He holds out his hand to Cashal. Cashal grabs it and jumps down. Cashal walks over to peek over the falls. Cutter jumps down to the ledge, followed by Camas.

"Damn." Cutter puts his hands on his knees in exhaustion, and both packs slide off his shoulders onto the ground.

Cashal walks over to pick up his pack. He bends down and grasps at it, missing. He grasps again and misses. "I see four packs!" he cries out.

"Cashal, you're delirious, man," Cutter says.

"Aye. Ma heid's mince."

"Christ. He needs to sit and rest for a bit. You two go ahead. I'll wait with this guy on the acid hit." Camas takes off her pack and sits down.

"I don't know, Camas. We should stick together," Reeve says.

"I need a little breather too. We'll be right behind you."

Cutter and Reeve lower themselves down the rock wall next to the waterfall, then down the trail along the river. Camas rests her head on her knees.

"Let's go, princess!"

Camas raises her head. "You need to rest a bit, big guy."

"The hell I do!" Cashal grabs his pack. As he staggers up, his foot catches a rock. He stumbles. Terror spreads over his face as his body falls back into the crest of the falls. Camas sees his feet upright at the brink.

"Heeeeeelp me!!"

Camas jumps up. "Fuck!!"

She quickly puts on her pack and lowers herself, grabbing zig-zag wood ladders and chains down the near-vertical trail. She sees Cashal bounce up at the bottom of the falls, his head down. His head lifts, buoyed by his soiled life vest. He bounces through the rough water, nearly getting pulled under the falls. His body travels for a distance, then slams into a rock, pinned by the water's force.

Camas reaches the bottom of the rock face and runs fast along the river. She gasps, unable to discern if his bowed head is in or out of the water. She leaps into the water, swims to Cashal, grabs onto the rock, and pulls his head up. She tries to free him from the rock, but the weight of the water carries too much force. Camas swims back to shore, reaches into her pack, and pulls out the z-drag kit. She anchors the line, assembles the prusik and pulleys, and swims back, fighting the force of the water. She reaches around Cashal with the rope, ties it securely, and swims back to shore.

Camas pulls with all her strength. The physics of the divided ropes overcomes the water's force, and Cashal dislodges. She pulls him in, grabs hold of his armpits, and drags him onto shore. His eyes are closed.

Camas leans down to breathe into his mouth. He doesn't revive.

Camas puts her mouth over Cashal's again. Nothing. "Damn you, you little Scottish Loch Ness monster. I didn't endure listening to your sexist jokes and control-freakdom this entire race to have you die on me!!"

Camas continues mouth-to-mouth resuscitation as persistently as her own heartbeat.

Cashal opens his eyes, coughs out some water. Camas lifts him in a firm hug.

"Ow. My leg," he says weakly. "Well, hello, beautiful mermaid," he slurs. "Look at your flowing locks, glimmerin' scales, fin, and tail," he says, looking at Camas from head to toe.

"You're delirious."

Cashal passes out. She firmly keeps her arms around him, then stands up and lifts him up and over her back. She groans as she lifts a leg to walk. Camas looks down the river. Step after step, she trudges with the weight of Cashal crushing her strong shoulders. Her breath heaves. Her steps are slow and steady. She struggles to find her footing as her mind and eyesight fog in the delirium of exhaustion.

Camas trips and falls to her knees. She cries out as she feels the rocks break skin. Cashal slumps down at her side.

Camas rolls Cashal onto his stomach. He groans. She moves on her knees to face his body, kneeling over his head. She thrusts her arms under his armpits and lifts one knee, blood dripping down her shin, then the other. She grunts as she stands up, Cashal's red hair pasted to his slumped head on her shoulder. She sticks her right leg through Cashal's, grabs his right hand with her left, and raises it to drape it over her shoulder. She bends her head under Cashal's armpit to stretch her arm around the back of his right knee.

"Whew, that's rank." The pungent body odor brings alertness as Camas squats strongly and shifts her shoulders to distribute his body weight on each side. She grabs Cashal's right hand with hers, looks up, then continues a steady march.

Camas begins a mantra taught to her by her best friend on the other side of the planet. "Sat nam. Sat nam," she repeats in the rhythm of her breath. "Sat nam. The truth is in me. Sat nam. Sat nam…"

Cashal groans. He hears the mantra and repeats it weakly along with her, "Sat nam. Sat nam. Sat nam."

Camas's steps become slower and slower, and the mantra slows with them. She stops with a heavy sigh. She tries to lift a leg. It won't budge. She begins to sob.

"I can't make it. I can't." Camas cries. The weight of Cashal is unbearable. She lets out a wounded cry and closes her eyes.

The air is silent except for the river gurgling next to them and Cashal continuing the mantra softly in his dreamlike state.

A hawk calls loudly.

Camas opens her eyes and sees a large red-tailed hawk sitting six feet in front of her. His talons grip a stack of race medallions. The bird watches her. Camas stares back and straightens. She raises her hand in a peace sign, lifts one foot heavily, then the next.

The bird opens its wings. Camas sees a cross in the form of a dark chestnut band on the top edge of its shoulders. She feels the air of the hawk's strong wings as it flaps powerfully, then rises into the air and flies over her.

Camas walks to the medallions and counts them quickly. Forty-nine. She takes one with her free hand. Mind now alert, she marches towards the Colorado River with her human pack and fingers gripping the Blueys' final medallion.

Camas comes around a bend in the trail and sees a dozen river rafts tied up in the distance close to the line of effervescent Tiffany-blue waters meeting chocolate-red silt rapids.

"Camas!" Reeve shouts as she appears with Cashal on her back.

Reeve and Cutter run at full speed to Camas.

"What happened?!" Reeve asks. "Stacey just brought us Cashal's pack. One of the camera crew found it!"

Cashal comes to. "I've long dreamed of this view of your arse," he says groggily.

Camas bends over, and Reeve takes Cashal off her back.

"Robert the Brute went over the falls." Camas undresses quickly and spreads her clothes on a rock. She stands in her sports bra and underwear. Reeve hands her a dry shirt, and Cutter finds dry shorts from his bag and brings them to her.

"Wow, that rescue was epic," Cutter says awkwardly, hugging her in her underwear.

Camas is silent and serious.

Reeve asks, "Are you OK?"

"I'm pretty sure I saw God out there."

Cashal growns in pain.

"And no, Cashal, it wasn't you."

CHAPTER 43
EIN GEDI, ISRAEL – 1,400 HA
(31.4664, 35.3880)

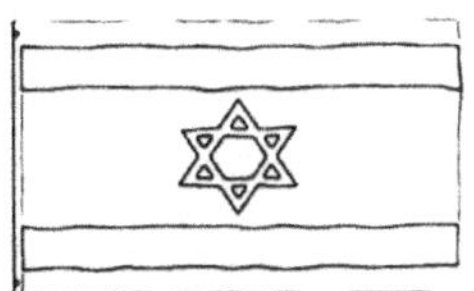

A race cameraman films the Blueys as they load their raft. Hare's chopper flies overhead with a cameraman filming.

"The Brave Blueys' captain, Cashal, injured his leg, and it looks like the team is discussing whether or not to continue. They're in second place behind the Blizzards. It would be a tragedy for them to lose their position with the Wildfires and Climatrons just a few miles behind."

"I think the ankle splint Stacey brought him should work," Reeve says, adjusting the velcro on the brace.

"I can finish... ow! ...the race."

"Of course, you can. No quitting now," Camas confirms. "By the way, captain, you missed the medallions when you were passed out." She pulls the medallion out of her bag and hands it to Cutter. "Maybe this is what you were swimming for."

Cutter and Reeve laugh.

Cashal looks at his map. "The first rapid is 164 Rapid. Looks like about seven river miles."

"I think Camas should captain from here," Cutter says, firmly holding the medallion in both hands.

Cashal and Camas are surprised.

"Cashal, you have enough to worry about staying out of the river with that leg. I agree with Cutter," Reeve says.

Cashal's head drops.

"I guess you're right." Cashal extends his arm very slowly, offering Camas the map, compass, and captain's phone. "Thanks for saving me."

"I only saved you because you're carrying my weed."

Cashal laughs weakly.

Camas walks over, takes the captain's tools from him, and hands him her phone. "Cashal, I'll just be your eyes on the map. I'll need your help, Red."

Cashal taps Camas's phone. "Any naked selfies on here?"

"I guess you're feeling better. Let's roll, Blueys!" Reeve says. "We need to make up some time."

Cutter holds the medallion out with both hands. The others put their hands on top of it.

"One, two, three," shouting, "Brave Blueys!" Their hands raise to the sky.

"Looks like the Blueys are continuing despite their captain's injury!" Hare announces.

The Blueys step into their raft and take hold of the oars. They look upward at the tall canyon walls as they pull out onto the fast-moving Colorado.

"That's Lava!" Cutter shouts. "Which side, captain?!"

"The left!" Camas calls. "The right has the hole! We'll

need to stay in the center of the left channel because there are rocks just under the water on either side!"

"Got it!" Cutter and Reeve shout.

"Aye!"

"We got this!" Camas shouts

"We're going to ride this mother to the win, lassie." Cashal smiles at her across the boat.

The water's roar envelopes the boat as the channel narrows closer to the churning froth.

"Whoo hoo!" Camas squeals. "Here we goooooo....!"

The Blueys march up a steep rocky trail along Diamond Creek, their faces and bodies marked with mud, blood, sweat, and tears, the camouflage of the canyon wilderness. Cutter leads the group, then Camas. They keep a respectable pace in the final push. Cashal lets out an occasional Gaelic groan as he limps tied with a rope behind Reeve.

"It's cooler, thank goddess."

"Not much," Cashal responds.

"I'll take ten degrees." Camas looks at the map. "We've climbed over 3,000 feet. We still have about two miles to go. It's the home stretch, Blueys."

"An donas dubh!! We didn't catch the Blizzards," Cashal shakes his head.

"We don't know where we'll place yet."

"We know they were in front of us. We didn't pass 'em."

"I saw some choppers earlier, but I don't see Hare's chopper. You'd think they'd be filming the finish." Cutter says.

"Maybe Hare's standing at the finish line," Reeve says.

"He's on the ground to give Cashal a big kiss," Camas teases.

"Reeve, untie me, mate. I can't be filmed tied to the rear like an asal."

Reeve unties him. "A what?"

"A donkey. Thanks for the carry, though. Appreciate it."

"You got it."

"Asal rhymes with Cashal," Camas says.

Cashal stares at Camas. A small smile forms through his sweat-caked upside-down red handlebar mustache and beard. He lets out a laugh. The laugh grows to a howl. The Blueys laugh hysterically, bent over as they hike, punch-drunk from twenty-one race days and nights.

They pick up the pace to a slow trot like horses returning to the stable. Cashal grunts as he hobbles to keep up as they follow along a dusty stream bed road. Old buildings, houses, and vehicles appear as they enter the small town of Peach Tree. Their heads turn left and right, searching for other teams, cameramen, and race crew.

"Look, there's a sign for Route 66 ahead!" Cutter says excitedly.

"Who the fuck cares, mate. Where are the crowds cheering us on?" Cashal asks, picking up speed.

"Stop!" Camas shouts.

Reeve and Cutter stop. Cashal keeps running.

"I'm the captain. Stop and get back here."

"What is it?!" Cashal hobbles back.

Camas looks at each of the guys. "Listen up. Whatever happens, wherever we place, I love you, stinky guys." Camas pulls them in for a hug. Cashal tries to put his head into her cleavage.

Camas pulls his head out. "Onward!"

The Blueys jog to arrive at Route 66. Cars whiz by in both directions. A car honks.

"Where's the god damn finish line?" Cashal says, frustrated. "What's the map say?"

"Peach Tree Route 66."

CHAPTER 44

CHIQUIBUL NATIONAL PARK, BELIZE – 106,839 HA

(16.8561, -88.7930)

The Blueys stand at the edge of Route 66. A bald eagle carved into a dramatic canoe-like extended roofline on the Hualapai roadside motel stares down at the wounded warriors.

The captain sat phone rings in Camas's pocket.

"It's Hare!" Camas shouts.

Cutter, Reeve, and Cashal gather around Camas.

"Cashal, put Camas on,"

"Cashal's injured. I have his phone. Camas. Over."

The phone beeps. Hare's stern face appears on the screen.

"I got a call from the Climatrons about your notes."

"What notes?" Camas asks, eyes upward to face the wooden eagle. Her mouth seals tightly and skews to the left of her face.

Her teammates are confused.

"You know what notes! Do you know how much this race cost to produce?!"

Camas is silent.

"$102 million!"

Silence.

"And now, instead of posting race footage of their adventures, athletes are filming gas wells, dirty mining ponds, and interviewing sick locals. Half the teams aren't even headed to the finish. What in the world were you thinking?!"

Silence.

"Camas, you better answer Hare," Reeve says.

"What were you thinking?!" Hare shouts.

She takes a slow drink of water, then wipes her brow with her forearm.

"What was I thinking?" Camas pauses.

"Yer bum's oot the windae. Answer him, lassie," Cashal encourages her gently.

Camas speaks firmly. She raises the phone directly in front of her face. "What was I thinking? You mean besides the fact that I should be drinking beer and smoking a joint with my hot boyfriend back in Sandglass rather than killing myself in this godforsaken race? What was I thinking? I'll tell you what I was thinking."

The Blueys' eyes are glued to Camas.

"I was thinking that the seventy-one percent black population of zip code 48217 in Detroit doesn't deserve to breathe the black air of a 250-acre tank farm or die fifteen years earlier than a white person in the suburbs in Gross Pointe Shores just a half-mile away. I was thinking that slavery isn't really dead in the eighty-file mile stretch of oil refineries called *cancer alley* in New Orleans where most of the folks are black and are fifty times more likely to develop cancer than you and me."

She gets louder. "I was thinking that we don't need a bigger pipeline leaking the dirtiest fossil fuel across the wild rice and watersheds of the Anishinaabe tribal lands and the 10,000 lakes of Minnesota."

The Blueys stand closer to her. Cutter puts his arm around her shoulder.

"I was thinking that the guardians of this magnificent Grand Canyon, the Havasupai, don't need another uranium mine in their back yard."

Hare is silent.

"And I was thinking that maybe this race could actually have something to do with the enviro-climate in its Enviro-Climate name!"

The line is silent.

"Roger that." Hare hangs up.

CHAPTER 45

MOUNT ARARAT NATIONAL PARK, TURKEY – 88,015 HA

(39.4287, 44.1756)

Camas shoves her phone in her pocket and looks at the guys. "Listen, I've been meaning to tell you someth…"

A low roar of engines is heard. The Blueys look around as the rumble grows louder and louder.

"What the hell?" Camas says as she walks along the front of the motel.

The Blueys follow the noise around the side of the building. Appearing like a mirage is the race teams, crew, Hualapai, and Havasupai tribal members in a large field. The Blueys walk like zombies towards the celebratory group who pack motorbike panniers, eat, drink, and mingle loudly.

An Australian voice sounds behind them. "Great race so far, Brave Blueys!!"

Camas, Reeve, Cutter, and Cashal turn. "So far?!!" they say in unison.

Three cameras flank Hare. Live music plays nearby.

"There's a change to the finish line of the race. After a mandatory rest night here, the race ends in Las Vegas at the

National People of Color Environmental Leadership Summit."

"The what?" Cashal asks.

The sky fills with stars as the Peach Tree Rascals croon and rap on a stage above the swaying and dancing athletes, crew, and locals. Sarah and Thomas sit in camp chairs in front of their CJ Camper. The Blueys dance in front of them.

"That shower felt amazing!" Cutter's lanky body moves to the music.

"You've got some moves, buddy. And look at your long hair!" Camas says, smiling as she dances skillfully with a sexy swagger. "And Reeve, look at you. You shaved!"

Reeve smiles, swaying to the band, beer in hand.

"How in the hell did we go from second place to the tail end?" Cashal asks as he rocks back and forth in a mock-jig.

"Hare provided mules, motorized rafts, choppers, and bikes to get everybody here. Teams that dropped out are back in too. They're meeting us at Lake Mead," Sarah answers from her chair.

"I started a Jesture group back in Hovenweep to chat with the teams."

Reeve and Cutter stop dancing.

"So that's why you were on your phone so much," Cashal says.

"We saw so much environmental shite during the race. Sarah and Thomas asked for help. Tilly called me to do something. Our friend Reina from the EPA did too."

"Why didn't you tell us?" Cutter asks, hurt. "Don't you trust us?"

"Oh, Cutter, of course, I trust you. I trust all of you."

Camas gets teary.

"Then how could we have gone through all of this together, and you kept it a secret?"

Camas tries to speak but is choked up. She swallows the lump in her throat.

"Camas felt that if you did your best, we would get all of those amazing shots, and if it caused even one person to take action to save the canyon, it would be worth it. She also didn't want to get you in trouble."

"Yer aff yer heid. One person would not be enough to make a difference."

"Those are bullshit reasons," Camas blurts.

Sarah is surprised.

"Sorry, Sarah. They're OK reasons, but I wanted to see what we could do. I wanted to prove I could do something as well as Tilly. I wanted to win."

Reeve, Cutter, Cashal, Sarah, and Thomas put their arms around her. A couple of other racers stop dancing and join the group hug. Cashal tries to flirt with one.

The smooth-voiced boy band, sons of Mexican, Filipino and Palestinian parents, sing, "I can't wait for you, to come my way, I've been far away, but I'll keep runnin', just to find a way to you 'til then."

The lead singer reaches down into the crowd and pulls up a young Hualapai local. He sings along, his voice blending beautifully with the colorful harmonies. *"My heart is like an open door, just ring me when you wanna go, I'll wait 'til you're home, hold a place 'til you're com-in' home, show you where the garden grows."*

Thomas leans over to kiss Sarah.

Camas taps her phone, "Hi baby, I miss you."

Rock formations tower on either side of the smooth blacktop as Hualapai and Havasupai men and women ride motorcycles alongside Parklands Enviro-Climate Challenge athletes.

Television cameras film as the sport and tribal brothers and sisters ride down the Las Vegas Strip, past the *Welcome to Fabulous Las Vegas* sign, to the Mandalay Bay Convention Center. TV crew in a helicopter films the two hundred rooftop solar panels and hordes of guests sunbathing around the 11-acre swimming pool.

Elders in traditional tribal dress lead the crowd of athletes on foot under the griffin guardians at the convention center entrance, where international team flags fly over a wide path to the finish line. Cheering spectators line the race route.

The Blueys have their arms around each other as they walk with the race procession.

Inside the immense convention center, a mock constitutional convention proceeds with testimonies, scientific presentations, sacred leader prayers, activist speeches, poets' words, artists' images, university scholar papers, newspaper reports, and personal and major TV network videos. The state representatives form a semi-circle at the front of hundreds of engaged attendees sitting in rows and standing around the halls' circumference.

Durga introduces the Secretary-General of the United Nations. He walks to the podium in front of a floor-to-ceiling jumbotron screen of a grid of live video of remote global environmental leaders next to the mock-constitutional convention representatives.

"The last decade was the hottest in human history, and these severe climate calamities weaken our political, economic, and social systems."

Kem Bullherder appears on the jumbotron. "I intended to be with you today, but I'm helping some friends in Liberia. Take heed!" Kem speaks passionately. "An environmental revolution is taking shape in the United States."

The crowd cheers.

"This revolution has touched communities of color from New York to California and from Florida to Alaska — anywhere where African Americans, Latinos, Asians, Pacific Islanders, and Native Americans live and comprise a majority of the population. Collectively, these Americans represent the fastest-growing segment of the population in the United States. They are also the groups most at risk from environmental problems."

Olivier Clan addresses the conference, "One: The federal government, states, and each person shall maintain and improve a clean and healthful environment for present and future generations. Two: The legislature shall provide for the administration and enforcement of this duty. Three: The legislature shall provide adequate remedies for the protection of the environmental life support system from degradation and provide adequate remedies to prevent unreasonable depletion and degradation of natural resources."

The crowd cheers.

Tilly appears on the screen behind Olivier. She wears a long dark blue silk longyi and a sky blue short-sleeve blouse. The sun shimmers off of her long silky black hair.

The crowd cheers. "Tilly! It's Tilly!"

"Thank you, Olivier. Thank you, scholars, leaders, and all proponents of the Green Amendment." She gives a friendly wave. Her beautiful smile fills the screen.

Tilly becomes serious. The crowd quiets.

"We are here for change."

The crowd cheers, and activists raise their banners.

"People, especially people of color, who have contributed the least to climate change, suffer its harms disproportionately. Air, water, fire, and cultural damage wreak havoc on our communities."

She walks to the edge of an outside terrace overlooking Lake Kandawgyi. The sacred Buddhist temple Shwedagon Pagoda is in the distance.

"We seek to end all forms of racial discrimination, but Mother Nature does not discriminate. The earth has been harmed, and all of us are paying the price. In this ancient city of Yangon, in a country named the second most vulnerable to climate change, Myanmar, the Global Climate Risk Index confirms that 'Signs of escalating climate change can no longer be ignored – on any continent or in any region.' Impacts from extreme-weather events hit the poorest countries hardest. We all see that superstorms, floods, landslides, cyclones, hurricanes, typhoons are occurring more frequently and more intensely."

Camas looks up at the towering griffin statue. "That bird is looking at me, and it's freaking me out."

"You just finished the toughest race in the world, and a rock spooks you?" Cashal asks.

"We're not across the finish line yet," Cutter reminds them.

"It looks like the bird that visited me after you were stuck in the rock."

"Your spirit bird?" Cashal teases.

"Maybe, but the bird didn't have a dinosaur head or a mohawk."

"Maybe it was a boobrie, the shapeshifting bird that inhabits the lochs in the west coast of Scotland."

"Boobrie? Well, of course, your mythological bird would be the boob."

The Blueys step up to the stack of finish-line medallions.

"One more time?" Camas asks.

The men nod.

"Cashal, will you go first?"

Cashal puts his hand on top of the medallion. Spectators, reporters, and TV cameras surround the Blueys. Camas puts her hand on top of Cashal's. Reeve and Cutter follow.

"One, two, three... Brave Blueys!!"

The crowd cheers. The four hug, laughing and crying.

Hare steps up and shakes their hands. "Good work, Blueys," he says.

"Thanks!" The Blueys turn to walk inside the hall.

"Hey, Camas," Hare calls.

Camas turns around.

"Great first race."

"Thanks! Good race for the enviro."

"Thank you."

A reporter jumps out, "Hey Camas, will you sign up for the next Enviro-Climate Challenge?"

"Fuck no!"

Hare shakes his head. Reeve, Cutter, and Cashal laugh. Cutter grabs her hand and pulls her to join them. The four continue walking arm in arm into the convention hall.

Camas points to the jumbotron. "Tilly!"

A few members of the audience turn to look.

"That's my best friend," Camas says to them. The Blueys find a spot along the back wall.

Reina walks up to Camas and hugs her. They turn back to watch Tilly.

"What is the Green Amendment? In basic terms, it means..." Tilly pauses, "... *no more Indian Givers.*"

The crowd cheers.

Tilly smiles. "Some of you who know me understand it. Camas nods. Some of you know it instinctively. Many have a hard time. Allow me to explain."

The crowd quiets.

"What you see behind me on the screen are the more than one hundred rollbacks of U.S. government regulations for environmental protections in just the last four years."

The crowd gasps.

The jumbotron screen splits to display the rollbacks one by one next to Tilly's image.

Tilly raises her right fist. Her voice is strong. "My beautiful people, my friends, among the one hundred rollbacks, thirty diminished protections for air quality!"

On the jumbotron:

Formally withdrew the United States from the Paris climate agreement, an international plan to avert catastrophic climate change adopted by nearly 200 countries.

Withdrew a Clinton-era rule designed to limit toxic emissions from major industrial polluters.

Revised a program designed to safeguard communities from increases in pollution from new power plants to make it easier for facilities to avoid emissions regulations.

"Nineteen of the rollbacks loosened protections of people living around oil and gas drilling!"

On the jumbotron:

Canceled a requirement for oil and gas companies to report methane emissions.

Relaxed Obama-era requirements for companies to monitor and repair leaks at oil and gas facilities, including exempting certain low-production wells – a significant source of methane emissions – from the requirements altogether.

Made significant cuts to the borders of two national monuments in Utah and recommended border and resource-management changes to several more.

Goosey Bitumines sits next to Bernard Lonely at a bustling white-tablecloth, dark wood-paneled steakhouse signing documents. She raises her red wine glass to meet Bernard's.

"There were rollbacks of fourteen rules related to our infrastructure and city planning and another sixteen rules that reversed protections for animals and biodiversity. Our clean water was threatened by the reversal of nine important rules. And twenty-four protections were rolled back in the area of other toxic substances!"

On the jumbotron:

Weakened the National Environmental Policy Act, one of the country's most significant environmental laws.

Revoked Obama-era flood standards for federal infrastructure projects that required the government to account for sea level rise and other climate change effects.

Revoked a directive for federal agencies to minimize impacts on water, wildlife, land, and other natural resources when approving development projects.

Tilly is silent. She closes her eyes and holds her hands in prayer pose. She opens her eyes and lowers her arms.

Her voice rises. "A family living on the edge of a mining field, a low-income housing project downwind of an industrial polluter, 100,000 square feet of Amazon distribution center spewing more pollution in census tracks with eighty-six percent people of color... *all* are multimillion dollar polluting enterprises against the individual. In the words of Robert D. Bullard, '...that playing field is not level, it is not fair.'"

The crowd cheers.

"And so, I ask you, how can we protect the earth, reverse climate change, and save all living things, including ourselves, if every time we make a change for the better, it is taken away just like all of the Indian Giver promises that were made to our Native American peoples?!"

The crowd stands and applauds loudly.

"Green Amendment now!!" Tilly raises her right fist to the sky.

"Green Amendment! Green Amendment!" the crowd chants to the rhythm of tribal drums.

CHAPTER 46
JABIL NATIONAL PARK, TUNISIA
– 150,000 HA

(33.0161, 9.1014)

Josh stands on the patio of Matchlove Brewery as the Blueys drive up. A jubilant Sandglass crowd cheers and raises their glasses as Camas leaps out of the car. She runs at full speed and jumps onto Josh, wrapping her legs around him, kissing him deeply.

Hare and Fiona sit in the front of their motorized raft, with Jamie at the rear steering the boat. The wind blows through their hair as the boat bounces over the sparkling blue waves. Hare answers his phone.

"Ha! I caught you!"

"Just barely, in one hundred yards, I'll be out of range of you," Hare says dryly. "Fremont, Whatcha got? You've got five seconds."

"The network called to congratulate you on the ratings and to ask where the next race will be."

Hare hangs up, puts his phone in his pocket, and pulls Felice in tightly for a kiss.

"Hare... Hare?... Hare!" Fremont stares at his phone.

Camas barges in the front door of Tilly and Liam's cottage. "Wake up, sleepyheads!" She walks into the bedroom. "Here are your coffees. Here are your maps and compasses."

Tilly is groggy. Camas sits on their bed, then lies on top of Tilly, kissing her hair. Liam laughs.

"I can't breathe," Tilly gasps, laughing.

"That's OK. You deserve it for making me worry!"

"Get off. I love you. Now, get off me!" Tilly laughs.

The three sit on the bed drinking coffee.

"Congratulations on the race. I'm so happy you survived."

Camas rolls her eyes. "Barely."

"And you made the top ten. That's amazing."

"We didn't win."

"I hear you worked to win something else."

"Word."

"Is that slang still used?"

"760 miles and the rankest man-stink. I'll use any damn slang I want. No offense, Liam."

"None taken." Liam smiles.

"Word. Did you miss me?"

"No."

Tilly and Liam laugh.

Camas puts her hands on her hips. "Get dressed, follow this map, and I'll see you at our new office in a couple of hours or a couple of days, depending on your planeteering skills."

"Ha! You're clever." Tilly examines the map. "We'll be there in under an hour!"

"I'll take P, so you don't have any excuses. I'll time you!

See you later, love birds." Camas rises from the bed. "I'm so happy you're home!" She runs out the door with Pedro.

Liam grabs Tilly and pulls her back into bed. "I'm so happy you're home too!" He kisses her.

"Nice work, darling. You and Thomas and your caravan made major tracks."

"Mom, we didn't get a real constitutional convention." Sarah's head sinks.

Durga hugs her daughter. "No, we didn't."

Sarah sobs into her mother's shoulder. A muffled sound emerges.

"What's that, my darling? I'm so proud of you, but I didn't understand you." She pauses, listening. "It's Ok. Don't worry. We did our best. You go ahead and cry."

Sarah cries louder. Her body is rhythmic against her mother. She stops, gasps for breath, her chest heaving. She inhales and looks into her mother's loving eyes. "Yet."

Tilly and Liam ride mountain bikes as they orienteer through Sandglass's tree-lined streets.

"It says '*Find a white spruce*.'" Liam says, looking at the map from Camas.

"Tilly, welcome home," Frill, a pretty barista with earspools and dreadlocks, says warmly.

"Thanks, Frill. Great to see you! Hey, Camas sent us on a hunt for a white spruce," Tilly says.

"That's one of our new custom blends."

"We'll take one!"

Tilly and Liam share the coffee as they walk around the

café, saying hello to friends, townspeople, and their dogs. The orienteerer-lovers wave goodbye and jump back on their bikes to continue the treasure hunt.

Find a huckleberry fish. Tilly and Liam ride through the Sandglass countryside to the Herd River Store. "One order of huckleberry pan-baked Idaho trout with warm lentil salad, please." They sit at a picnic table by the river and enjoy the local delicacies

Ride a ski chair lift. Tilly and Liam ride up Schweitzer Mountain road. They buy two lift tickets, load their bikes onto the chair lift, then take the next chair. At the top, the attendant unloads their bikes, they ride to share a pint of MickDuff's Lupulicious at Sky House, then ride their bikes down the mountain trail.

Kiss a symbol of freedom and each other. Tilly and Liam ride to the City Beach Statue of Liberty sculpture. Liam steps onto her concrete base and strains to reach the statue's lips. Tilly gives him a boost. He kisses the Idahoan lady liberty, jumps down, pulls Tilly in, and kisses her.

Drink a Grateful Dead heavenly elixir. Tilly and Liam walk into Bijou Nez Winery and share a glass of Deadhead Red Petit Verdot.

Find a radish bouquet. Tilly and Liam walk through the Sandglass Farmer's Market and buy a bunch of radishes. Liam goes down on one knee and presents the bouquet treasure to his bride.

Eat garlic with Donald Duck. Tilly and Liam park their bikes in front of Letera 22. They snap a photo of the soft head Donald Duck Pez dispenser, the most valuable in the vast collection, as they eat a plate of garlic fries.

Find Bachelorettes Barge Club.

"What in the world?" Liam says, popping a mint.

"Aw, now I can't kiss you because your breath is fresh, and I'm still garlicky," Tilly says.

Liam pulls Tilly in for a kiss. "Oh, wait. I know that Bachelors Barge Club is the oldest boathouse in the U.S."

"How in the world do you know that?"

"My dad likes rowing and history."

"That's it! Must be the new office. Let's go!"

Tilly and Liam ride up to the rowing club building with wide eyes and smiles. Camas stands outside, looking at her watch. She is barefoot, wearing an all-white linen caftan and white yoga pants.

"Two hours thirteen minutes," Camas says.

"Is this it?" Tilly asks excitedly. "Wow! And look at you all guru-goddessed out!"

"I'm spiritual now."

"Oh?"

"Come check it out!" Camas leads them up the stairs.

"We had a blast, by the way. It was so fun seeing everyone as we orienteered around town on the bike-only lanes that Mayor Patrick has finished."

"I thought you would," Camas smiles at her best friend as they enter an old wood building with high exposed wood rafters and huge warehouse windows facing the sparkling deep blue lake.

"Cool space," Liam says, looking around.

"Cam, it's amazing! Look at that view. I'm not sure I'll get any work done because I'll be wanting to get on the lake."

"That's OK. I'm doing all the work anyway," she teases.

They laugh.

"Till, we need to rescue Dad and Liz from P," Liam reminds Tilly.

"Would you mind picking him up? I'd like to hang out here for just a bit more."

"No problem," Liam says, kissing her. He kisses Camas on the cheek. "Nice find, Cam."

Tilly and Camas walk outside to a deck overlooking the water. A couple of people pull their shells out of the water into the boathouse and wave a hello.

"I love the high ceiling and big windows, but won't the office be expensive to heat?"

"I thought of that too. We have a solution."

"What is it?"

"Remember that day in Reykjavic when you had to be a polar bear and swim in the cold water when everyone else in Iceland swims in thermal-heated water?"

"I remember."

"Well, I met an older man having a beer in the pub who has a cool invention. He was in Iceland showing it to that Perla lady."

"Perla Seruma."

"Yeah, her. It takes centripetal force from the motion of water to generate energy. He says it runs by itself, but if you want to have even more energy, you can walk on top of it."

"So, if I went on a little meditative walk around it, or we walked in circles around it when we were meeting, it would generate even more power?"

"That's pretty much it. He knows your work and offered to build it at no charge."

"That sounds like magic."

"I didn't mention it before because I wasn't sure if we could find a lakefront place. We just need to be willing to let others see the swirlamajig. I told him it needed music too."

"That'll be no problem. Letting folks see it, that is. You scored on this place."

Camas pulls Tilly down onto a yoga mat, and they sit in lotus position overlooking the lake. They close their eyes and meditate.

Tilly opens her eyes and looks around. "This place gives us room to grow."

"Our non-profit status was approved."

"Wow, Cam, that's so exciting. And, there's room for a kids play area."

"Sure. I don't think too many visitors will bring their toddlers, but you never know."

Tilly puts her arm around her, then takes her hand and puts it on her belly.

"What!? Really?!" Camas says, grabbing Tilly in an embrace. "I could have squished the baby this morning! Why didn't you tell me then?"

Camas jumps up, pulling Tilly up with her. She changes the yoga music to an upbeat rock song. She takes Tilly's hands, and they dance on the deck.

"I'm waiting for the right time to tell Liam," Tilly says over the music. "He's been preoccupied with Graeme's surgery. You can't spoil the beans. Promise."

"I promise," Camas says with a big smile, hugging Tilly again. "Auntie Camas can keep a secret. I'll have lots of secrets that your baby will tell me that we'll keep from you."

"I'm sure." Tilly laughs.

"How's Josh?"

"Gorgeous as ever, inside and out." Camas pauses. "And he told me he missed me."

"Of course, he did." Tilly smiles.

CHAPTER 47
PATUCA NATIONAL PARK, HONDURAS – 375,584 HA

(14.4321, -85.4463)

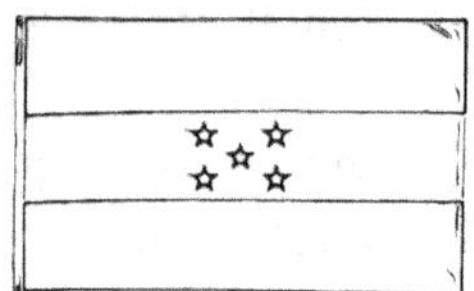

Pedro lies next to Tilly as she sits in padmasana with her eyes closed on top of a grassy knoll in the center of the sacred grounds outside Sandglass. The warm breeze blows through the trees, and Tilly's long black hair floats in the air like a spider's silk threads ballooning through the air on earth's electricity.

"Ancestors," Tilly whispers. "I ask your help to reconcile my voyage."

Birds sing, and clouds move slowly over the tall pines. Pedro is alert. He surveys the landscape, moving his head back and forth to follow squirrels and butterflies.

Pedro barks. He runs down the hill and disappears into a field of tall white, fluffy plumes of beargrass.

"P! P, come!"

Pedro doesn't turn around. Tilly stands up from her meditation and follows him.

"P!" Tilly calls as she runs down the hill through the long grass that her ancestors used for baskets, braids, dress fringe, necklaces, and quivers. She jumps over old fallen trees and stones.

Pedro digs in the earth at the bottom of a ravine.

"What are you doing?!" Tilly calls.

Pedro digs frantically, dirt flying up behind him.

Tilly walks closer. Pedro digs and digs. She looks closer and sees the top of a stone. Tilly gets down on her knees and scrapes dirt away alongside Pedro. The large stone is round and smooth. Pedro and Tilly continue digging.

They stop for a moment. Pedro looks up at Tilly.

"Oh my goodness, that's it. You've found the Peace Stone, clever P."

"P, stay." Tilly gets out of her white 1978 Toyota longbed pickup truck, runs into her cottage, races past Liam, and rummages through a cabinet. "Hi!" she shouts, her head down.

"How were your hike and meditation? Where's P?"

Tilly doesn't answer as she vigorously moves books, wrapping papers, small boxes, and garden tools as she mumbles incoherently.

"What in the world are you looking for? Can I help you?" Liam asks.

"Yes, please! I'm looking for some rope. Oh, here it is! Can you find a tarp? That one we use for camping's OK."

Liam quickly finds the tarp. Tilly runs out of the house, rope in hand, and hops into her truck. "Get in!"

"What's going on?"

"I'll show you when we get there."

Tilly, Liam, and Pedro hike to the sacred grounds. Liam follows Tilly and Pedro as they run down the hill. Tilly spreads out the tarp. They use a thick branch to lever the stone out of the dirt hole and roll it onto the tarp. They wrap the tarp around the heavy stone, tie it with the rope, then both take a rope end to pull it slowly, little by little up the hill, stopping to rest at intervals.

Pedro tries to help, so Liam finds a branch and breaks it into a one-foot-long piece. He ties a section of the rope to it. Pedro takes the wood in his mouth and pulls. The three struggle to drag the tarp and stone to the top of the hill. "Heave ho! Heave ho!"

Tilly stands at the former site of the stone. "P, come! Dig!" She points to a soft place and shows him by digging herself. Pedro digs. Tilly and Liam help him until they create a concave cavity. They lever the stone again to rest at the top of the sacred mound once more.

Liam and Tilly sit facing each other, their legs entwined over the stone.

"Thanks for helping me," Tilly says as she looks down at the round stone. She puts her hands wide on top as if warming them. She takes Liam's hands and puts them on the stone, then takes them and puts them on her belly. He looks up at her with wide eyes.

"Oh my God!" Liam says with a huge smile. "Are you…?"

"Yes."

"I can't believe I let you pull this stone up the hill or travel to Liberia!"

"Let me?" she teases.

"You know what I mean," he says, leaning over the stone to embrace and kiss her.

"Liam, there's something discovered on my journey and didn't even realize until P found the Peace Stone."

"What?"

"Green *is* peace. And peace *is* green."

Liam sits thinking.

Tilly continues, "The countries that are the most green are also the countries with the most peace. On the opposite spectrum are the countries in war. Those countries have the most environmental degradation."

"Wow. It makes sense. Why has no one told us that?"

"I think one reason is that the warring countries are just too embroiled in violence to peek out of the muck to see the light."

"Hmmm."

"And then there are those who know, who profit from the violence, and the resources being pillaged. That's the vice grip. If we can stop the violence, change could happen."

"Sounds impossible."

"I'll make very few requests of you in our life together, but one is that I never hear those words out of your mouth again, please," she says with a loving smile.

"Sounds like a challenge. World peace."

"Think about it. It's the key that unlocks everything. It's like walking through to another dimension. By bringing peace to all people, we save the planet too. By slowing down to carbon negative, we bring peace." Tilly holds up her right hand in a peace sign.

Liam holds his right hand in a peace sign and rests it on her belly. They kiss tenderly.

CHAPTER 48

MASOALA NATIONAL PARK, MADAGASCAR – 240,500 HA

(-15.6476, 50.1009)

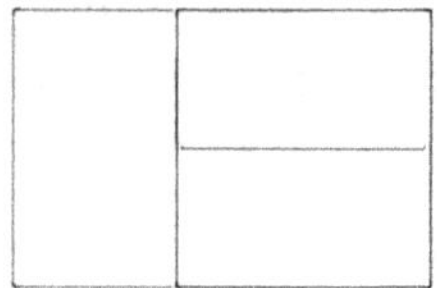

"Remember when you told me I should stop swimming so fast?" Tilly says to her friend Ike, an older, grey-bearded man with tan leathery skin, who wears a cloth baby diaper hat on his head.

"I have a feeling you and that little one will be swimming pretty darn fast."

Camas and Liam walk up on either side of Tilly and stretch a piece of yarn out around their waists, trying to guess how much it would take to go around Tilly's belly in the classic baby shower game.

Frida, with long grey hair and deep-set wrinkles in her olive skin, walks up. She carries a wicker basket covered with a pretty colored napkin, and her husband, Bear, holds a huckleberry pie in one hand and a vintage ice cooler in the other.

"Huckleberry pie!" Ike exclaims. "Let me help you."

"Here's a host gift for you," Frida says, kissing Ike on the cheek. She hands him a bottle-shaped gift.

The old friends catch up as they arrange food on the buffet table.

"How was Burma?" Bear asks. Bear, 6'5", towers over

Frida. His rolled-up flannel shirt reveals black ink on one arm in an art-culture blend of Day of the Dead to Native American to Samoan.

"Wait," Frida says, walking over and grabbing Tilly's hand. "I want to hear too! What was your favorite place?"

"I could never pick. The most dramatic scenery might have been Iceland, but Myanmar reminded me of the Selkirks in low light, where the peaks are ancient spires. Then, of course, there's P's homeland, Portugal," Tilly says, petting Pedro.

The group chuckles.

"I've always known in my heart that peace is possible, but I think I carried it with me intellectually as a hope, not a belief. Does that make sense?"

Frida holds her hand. "Yes, dear one."

"Now I know it is possible in our lifetime."

"Maybe your lifetime, not mine," Ike jokes.

"No, Ike," she says thoughtfully.

"But doesn't that make perfect sense that if we have been waging war on the environment, there could never be a way to be a peaceful world?" Bear says solemnly.

Pedro runs over to the picnic table and sniffs the Huckleberry pie. He jumps to put his paws on the table.

"P, no!"

He jumps off and runs over and puts his snout on Tilly's pregnant belly.

"He usually obeys so well. Lately, he is very needy."

Frida hands Tilly a small present. "I got this for you a month ago."

Tilly looks lovingly at the three of them. "You three are among the most important people in my life. After Mom and Dad died, I don't know what I would have done without you." Tilly looks at the present. "What is this?"

"Open it."

Tilly unwraps the paper and opens the box. Inside is a pair of beaded baby moccasins.

"You already knew!" Frida and Tilly have a sweet hug.

Tilly sits with presents and friends surrounding her. Liz hands Tilly a present, and Graeme hands one to Liam. Tilly unwraps a baby life jacket, and Liam unwraps a baby wetsuit. They hold the gifts up to their friends, laughing.

The shower guests grimace as they sample baby food masked in paper bags.

Pedro lays his chin on Tilly's belly.

Josh, Cutter, Joe, and Reeve, also known as The Bike Guys, gift Tilly, and Liam a small wooden no-wheels toddler bike.

Tilly and Camas sit on the same side of a picnic table facing Lake Bijou Nez. Tilly is silent.

"You sounded pretty discouraged when you were in Africa. It must have gotten even worse in Asia. Are you still discouraged?" Camas asks.

"Despite the darkness, there was an incredible amount of light. I saw an African fig tree creeping through the cracks and crevices of a one-hundred-year-old crumbling colonial building. It seemed to be saying, despite your attempts to control and harm me, I embrace you. I hold you up. There is hope." Tilly pauses. "And Sapo National Park is monitoring pygmy hippos."

"I think I would like tiny hippos."

"You would," Tilly smiles.

An Ivorian boy rides his bike along the road bordering the Akouédo dump landfill in Abjidan. Birds fly over straw blankets and wattles as oyster and turkey tail mushrooms emerge energetically in a fast forward time-lapse of restoration.

A box of diamonds sits next to a middle-aged man at an antique wood table. He places a diamond onto a tiny scale, then holds the diamond in one hand and a monocular loupe to his eye in the other, looking carefully under the light. He marks down quality details on a piece of paper, then puts the paper and the diamond in a small envelope.

Hurricane winds and seawater crash into Sylvan Beach Pavilion and a neighborhood of small houses in a coastal Texas town.

Camas hands Tilly a present. The baby shower guests laugh and chatter in the distance.

"What's this? You already got me those cute One More Year onesies."

"Just open it."

Tilly sets the present on the picnic table and opens the box. Inside is a folded board and many colorful pieces shaped like animals, birds, fish, and plants in different shades of green.

"It's your board game!"

"Our board game. The pieces are species that are nearly extinct. They're too small for the baby, but eventually, she'll be big enough to play with us."

"She?"

"I just have a feeling."

Tilly smiles. "Well, if it's a boy, hopefully, he'll be girly."

"A girly boy would be perfect too."

"I love that the pieces aren't plastic. It even has a compass. It's great, Cam!" Tilly hugs Camas.

"The pieces are made in Sandglass."

Tilly studies the game carefully, picking up the pieces. "You know, I realized that green is the same as peace."

"Of course, it is."

Tilly lets out a belly laugh.

"There you have it. It needed a name," Camas says.

"What's the name?"

"Peace of Green."

"Brilliant, friend."

Camas puts her arm around Tilly and holds two small wooden game pieces in the shape of a tree and a hippo on her belly as they look out over Lake Bijou Nez.

THE END

PEDRO'S PRIMER

Tilly asked me to share a few woofs with you.

Two days ago, which is two weeks ago in your human time, I was lying at my mistress Tilly's feet. She thought I was asleep because my eyes were closed after a long hike in Sherwood Forest. I wasn't sleeping. I was listening to her voice. I love her voice, even when she's mad at me. Sometimes I chew something up, and she gets louder. But I know she loves me, and I love her.

As her smooth voice was bouncing over my curls and into my ears, I heard the words, "If we can make a picture of it, we can make it so."

I perked up. I could see a picture of my best friend, Roxie. I could see a big bowl of kibble with some wild salmon treats sprinkled on top.

Then I heard her say, "If we can picture peace on earth, it can be so."

The next day, Roxie showed up to run with us, and when we got home, I had a big bowl of kibble with salmon treats on top.

And so, I'm pretty sure she knows what she's talking about.

I think peace *is* possible if we love dogs more.

$$\mathcal{P}$$

PEDRO DE SOUSA SARAMAGO MEGELLAN

AFTERWORD

"Our words are our prayers, our sound is our song, and our power is the drumbeat. When we do all that, the wind carries that everywhere, all over the world,"
Havasupai elder Richard Watahomigie

"Environmental justice requires that we, as individuals, make personal and consumer choices to consume as little of Mother Earth's resources and to produce as little waste as possible; and make the conscious decision to challenge and reprioritize our lifestyles to ensure the health of the natural world for present and future generations."
Principle #17 of the Principles of Environmental Justice
and #1 Principle of *One More Year. Keep your stuff longer, people.*

Principles of Environmental Justice
The First National People of Color Environmental
Leadership Summit
24–27 October 1991 Washington, DC

PREAMBLE

AFTERWORD

We, The People of Color, gathered together at this multinational People of Color Environmental Leadership Summit to begin to build a national and international movement of all
peoples of color to fight the destruction and taking of our lands and communities, do hereby
re-establish our spiritual interdependence to the sacredness of our Mother Earth, respect and
celebrate each of our cultures, languages and beliefs about our natural world and our roles in
healing ourselves; to insure environmental justice; to promote economic alternatives which
would contribute to the development of environmentally safe livelihoods; and to secure our
political, economic and cultural liberation that has been denied for over 500 years of colo-
nization and oppression, resulting in the poisoning of our communities and land and the
genocide of our peoples, do affirm and adopt these principles of Environmental Justice:

1. Environmental justice affirms the sacredness of Mother Earth, ecological
   unity and the interdependence of all species, and the right to be free from
   ecological destruction.

2. Environmental justice demands that public policy be based on mutual
   respect and justice for all peoples, free from any form of discrimination or
   bias.

3. Environmental justice mandates the right to ethical, balanced, and
   responsible uses of land and renewable resources in the interest of a
   sustainable planet for humans and other living things.

4. Environmental justice calls for universal protection from nuclear testing and
   the extraction, production, and disposal of toxic/hazardous wastes and
   poisons that threaten the fundamental right to clean air, land, water, and
   food.

5. Environmental justice affirms the fundamental right to political, economic,
   cultural, and environmental self-determination of all peoples.

6. Environmental justice demands the cessation of the production of all toxins,
   hazardous wastes, and radioactive materials and that all past and current
   producers be held strictly accountable to the people for detoxification and
   the containment at the point of production.

7. Environmental justice demands the right to participate as equal partners at
   every level of decision-making, including needs assessment, planning,
   implementation, enforcement and evaluation.

8. Environmental justice affirms the right of all workers to a safe and healthy

work environment without being forced to choose between an unsafe livelihood and unemployment. It also affirms the right of those who work at home to be free from environmental hazards.

9. Environmental justice protects the right of victims of environmental injustice to receive full compensation and reparations for damages as well as quality health care.

10. Environmental justice considers governmental acts of environmental injustice a violation of international law, the Universal Declaration of Human Rights, and the United Nations Convention of Genocide.

11. Environmental justice must recognize a special legal and natural relationship of Native Peoples to the U.S. government through treaties, agreements, compacts, and covenants affirming sovereignty and self-determination.

12. Environmental justice affirms the need for an urban and rural ecological policies to clean up and rebuild our cities and rural areas in balance with nature, honoring the cultural integrity of all our communities and providing fair access for all the full range of resources.

13. Environmental justice calls for the enforcement of principles of informed consent, and a halt to the testing of experimental reproductive and medical procedures and vaccinations on people of color.

14. Environmental justice opposes the destructive operations of multi-national corporations.

15. Environmental justice opposes military occupation, repression, and exploitation of lands, peoples and cultures, and other life forms.

16. Environmental justice calls for the education of present and future generations which emphasizes social and environmental issues based on our experience and an appreciation of our diverse cultural perspectives.

17. Environmental justice requires that we, as individuals, make personal and consumer choices to consume as little of Mother Earth's resources and to produce as little waste as possible; and make the conscious decision to challenge and reprioritize our lifestyles to ensure the health of the natural world for present and future generations.